The St. Valentine's Day Cookie Massacre

(A Hatter's Cove Gazette Mystery)

Elisabeth Crabtree

Copyright © 2014 by Elisabeth Crabtree

All rights reserved. No part of this book may be reproduced without the written permission of the author.

ISBN-13: 978-1495384462
ISBN-10: 1495384462

First Printing, February 2014
v. 4.6.14

Book cover designed by San at http://www.coverkicks.com/

Illustrations: www.Bigstock.com

AUTHOR'S NOTE

This is a work of fiction. Names, characters and situations are completely fictional and a work of the author's imagination. Any resemblance to any person, living or dead is purely coincidental.

Other books by Elisabeth Crabtree

Books in the Grace Holliday Cozy Mystery Series:
Deadly Magic
Deadly Reunion
Death Takes a Holiday
Murder Games

Books in the Hatter's Cove Mystery Series:
St. Valentine's Day Cookie Massacre

CHAPTER ONE

"I LOST TEN pounds," I said as I dropped into the chair next to my editor's desk and glared. I tried not to take it personally when he cringed as he looked up.

Hayden Reese, publisher and editor of the Hatter's Cove Gazette and my chief annoyance at the moment, albeit a very handsome annoyance, but an annoyance just the same, smiled brightly. "Kat, what are you complaining about? People would kill to have your job tasting all the best cuisine our fine town has to offer. Weren't you in here two weeks ago complaining about gaining ten pounds? I would think that most people would be happy to have lost the weight they had gained."

"Yes, after a couple of months with some moderate dieting and exercise, most people would be happy." I nodded agreeably before pounding my fist on the desk between us. "They would not be happy to lose it all at once over a two day period after eating at Mack's All You Can Eat Crab Shack. This is the third bout of food poisoning I've had since moving back home." I held up my hands. "I'm done. I'm not eating anymore."

He gave me a long-suffering sigh. "You are our food columnist. That means you must eat at our local restaurants."

My stomach rumbled at the mere mention of such a threat. "I had to have my stomach pumped." I leaned forward and stared intently into his green eyes. "I think they're trying to poison me."

Hayden chuckled as he ran a hand through his already tousled light brown hair. "Oh, don't be ridiculous."

"Oh no?" I stood and motioned for him to follow me to my desk. A few seconds later, I thrust a dozen or so poison pen letters under his nose.

He propped his hip against my desk and began leafing through the letters and email printouts. "What is this?"

"My fan mail."

"You don't deserve to eat ever again," he read. "Your palate, like your opinion, is utter rubbish, and should be relegated to the trash heap much like that rag of a paper you work for." He dropped the letter down on my desk. "That's nice."

I tucked my brown hair behind my ears, and leaned over his shoulder. I tapped at the sheet of paper in his hand. "That's from the Ugly Swan Pub." I felt a smile tug at my lips. "I said their trout had all the flavor of an old tire, but was harder to chew."

Hayden shuffled through the letters, only stopping when he came across an eight by eleven sheet of paper. He frowned and ran a thumb across the words, *I hope you choke to death*, which had been cut out of magazines and pasted to the sheet. "Well, maybe you should consider toning down your piece just a tad."

"I'm not a food critic," I said, for what seemed like the thousandth time since the gazette's former food critic left to join a rival paper the month before. "I'm an investigative journalist."

"You know we're short handed. Everyone has to pitch in and take columns they wouldn't necessarily do until we're up to full strength again." His eyes widened as he continued to read my mail.

"I don't mind pitching in. I would just rather do something a little less dangerous or unhealthy, like writing a column on swimming with sharks or wrestling alligators. You know, something safer."

"As soon as we hire another critic, you won't ever have to eat at another restaurant as long as you live, but for now, you will be handling the food columns. You know, no one else would take it and since you were our newest hire, you got stuck with it."

"Just my luck." *If I had only known*, I thought in amusement. Truth was I would have taken the job regardless. A few months ago, I decided to leave Miami and return to my old hometown. Miami had been nice, but after ten years, I had gotten tired of the big city, and wanted to find something a bit cozier and laid back. To be honest, I had started to get homesick. There was just something about Hatter's Cove. Therefore, at my family's urging, I put in my notice at one of Miami's finest papers, packed my bags, and moved back home with the intention of helping my family out at the family business, and possibly doing some freelance work during the slow times. I was really looking forward to a life of peace and quiet.

I just didn't realize how quiet Hatter's Cove was, or how slow time could actually move here and two weeks of mind-numbing, soul-crushing peace and quiet later, I found myself at the Gazette's door, looking for a job. During my last year of high school, I had interned at the Gazette and had fond memories of the place. I glanced up at Hayden through my lashes. *And the people.*

I had been interning at the Gazette only one week when Hayden arrived in town, much to the excitement of our then editor-in-chief who was looking for a good reporter. Hayden had made a name for himself up north and had followed some girl he was in love with to Hatter's Cove. She left, but he stayed, much to our editor's delight and mine. I quickly developed quite the crush on our new star reporter. He was handsome, strong, smart, dedicated, and genuinely nice and caring. Unfortunately, he was a whole five years older than I was, and to him, I was just a gangly high schooler that he had to take under his wing. He was nice and patient, but so very uninterested. I left after graduation for greener pastures, wondering if I would ever see him again. Now, granted, I didn't pine away for him after I left, but I didn't exactly forget about him either.

So, it was a pleasant surprise to discover that, not only was he still at the Gazette, but that he had recently purchased the paper, and was now its publisher as well as owner. It was a less pleasant surprise to discover that the Gazette, a hundred year institution in Hatter's Cove, was in dire straits.

A few months before I arrived, a new paper, the Hatter's Cove Herald, opened its doors and systematically began trying to crush their competition. Within a few weeks they had poached the majority of the Gazette's staff. One by one, the Gazette's reporters, copy editors, and sales staff left for the Herald, leaving only a handful of employees left. They had tried to get Hayden to join them but he had other plans. Apparently, after everyone had abandoned ship, the last owner was quick to abandon as well and sold the paper to Hayden for far less than it was worth. The Gazette was almost shut down as a result, but Hayden kept it running against all odds. Despite the Herald's interference, he was able to hire other reporters to fill most of the vacant spots. Therefore, two months after the exodus, I showed up at the Gazette's door just to see if there were any openings. Little did I know that, the moment I walked through the door, I would be hired. I would like to believe it was based on my stellar reputation, or at least his equally fond memories of me, but I'm not that delusional. The sad truth was that he was desperate. With no more than a brief glance at my resume, Hayden thrust the life section of the paper in my hands and told me they needed someone to cover the latest dog show. In five minutes.

In three months, I had covered every dog, cat, bird show, restaurant opening, and craft show that the town had put on. When I wasn't doing that, I was penning the food columns. Not exactly, the features I had become accustomed to writing in Miami, but beggars couldn't be choosers. I sat down in my chair and surveyed our office. My eyes fell on a book of puzzles. "What about the crossword puzzle? I'm good at puzzles."

"Beatrix would kill you and me if we took the crossword puzzle from her and gave it to you. I think she's starting to enjoy it."

I glanced over at one of the other reporters in the office. Simon Sayors looked away from his computer screen long enough to roll his eyes at me. I schooled my features. Beatrix Allen, the Gazette's Queen Bee, as the other reporters refer to her, usually behind her back, had proven to be a thorn in my side since I joined the Gazette three months ago. She spent the majority of her time flitting in and out, leaving general unhappiness wherever she went. She should have been fired long ago, but Hayden was nothing if not loyal. She and Simon, the Gazette's intern at the time, were the only members of the staff, besides

Hayden, that had remained after the others had left and Hayden was determined to reward them for their loyalty.

I leaned back in my chair and glanced out the window. "Who's covering the courthouse Monday morning?"

"I'm going to let Simon handle it." He waved a careless hand toward the young man sitting a few desks away playing computer solitaire.

Simon whipped his head around. He gave me a panicked look before turning back around to his game. After everyone jumped ship, Simon had been suddenly promoted from intern to full-fledged reporter. Desperate times merit desperate measures and all that. Nevertheless, despite being friendly and eager, he was still rough around the edges and had a tendency to panic at the slightest thing. So far, he had been assigned small things to cover, but it looked like Hayden was ready to send him out on his own. Clearly, it was whether Simon wanted it or not, and by the terrified look Simon just gave me, I had a feeling that he didn't want to be set loose just yet.

"On his own?" I asked.

"He's ready."

I could see Simon silently shaking his head out of the corner of my eye. "Simon's still young." Wincing at how that sounded, I glanced back at Simon. "No offense."

Without looking up from his computer, Simon raised his hand. "None taken."

Hayden glanced my way. "You're not exactly an old lady."

My lips quirked up slightly. "I'm glad you noticed." I had started to wonder if I was losing my touch. While in my early thirties and still fit, three months sampling every type of fried concoction ever invented, had begun to take its toll on my figure. *What sort of monster had decided to fry candy bars and make it a dinner selection, and why were all the restaurants in town suddenly specializing in this vile creation?* I thought as I glanced down at my legs.

A furtive motion out of the corner of my eye caught my attention. I glanced over at Simon who was trying to hide a comic book underneath his faded blue Willie's Bait Shop t-shirt. He leaned back quickly and ran a hand over his floppy, sandy blond hair, and tried rather unsuccessfully to look completely nonchalant. I leaned over and looked to the door.

Right on time.

Rosie Lopez, our sports writer and one of Hayden's first hires after the mass exodus breezed in with barely a glance toward Simon. Rosie, to her friends, had quite the impressive resume. She not only held a degree in journalism but she was also an Olympic beach volleyball silver medalist. From what I understood, it was quite the coup when Hayden wooed her away from the Herald. She gave us a cherry hello as she threw her duffle bag onto the desk.

"How was it, Rosie?" Hayden asked.

"Horrible," she said. "The Mad Hatter's lost by fifty-five points. By half time, the other team felt so bad they started hanging back and 'accidentally' dropping the ball. That still didn't help."

"Did they at least make a goal this time?" I asked.

Rosie nodded. "Absolutely."

"Good," Hayden said, "at least the streak is over." He picked up another letter and began to read.

Rosie unzipped her duffle bag. "It was for the opposing team."

"So, basically it went better than last time," I said brightly. At Rosie's questioning glance, I added, "At least they scored this time."

"Progress." Rosie glanced at her wrist. "I'll write something up tonight. I just came by to drop off my bag. I have another game to go to."

Simon leaned forward excitedly. "Would you like some help? I used to be quite an athlete when I was in middle school."

Hayden glanced up from my death threats. "War of Warcraft doesn't count, kid."

Simon ignored him. "I could help you follow the game. Take notes."

"Sorry, sweetie, it's just a private volleyball game between friends on the beach," she said. "I won't be writing it up."

"Oh." Simon leaned back in disappointment, as Rosie pulled out a bathing suit, flip-flops, and sunscreen from her duffle bag.

She glanced over at me. "What's the temperature out there today?"

I didn't even bother checking my phone's weather app. "It's Valentine's Day in South Florida. I'm sure it's a brisk, chilly, 85 degrees."

"I better get my parka," Rosie said as she strolled out of the office. I couldn't help but notice that Simon's shoulders slumped as he turned back to his solitaire game.

As a sudden thought occurred to me, I plastered a helpful smile on my face. "I'd be happy to go to the courthouse with Simon. Take him under my wing, so to speak."

Still glancing through the various death threats by unhappy restaurant owners, and one exceedingly polite, but angry letter from the tourism commission, Hayden said, "That's what I'm afraid of. Chief Waltrip almost arrested you last week for obstruction."

"Almost doesn't count. He didn't have any evidence and he knew it." With a sigh, I rose to my feet. I needed coffee if I was ever going to get through this day. Valentine's Day when single, left much to be desired. Spotting the coffee pot in the corner of the room, thankfully filled to the brim, I made my way over to my version of black gold.

Hayden tossed the letters back on my desk. "I do have a new assignment for you though."

"Really?" I asked without much enthusiasm, as I poured several packets of sugar into my coffee. I stirred the sugar in and carefully brought the cup to my mouth, blowing on it to cool it down some. "What is it this time?"

"Someone has personally requested your presence at their grand opening."

Surprised, I snorted. Unfortunately, I had just taken a drink of my coffee, which set off a series of less than ladylike hacks. "Who?" I squeaked out between gulps of air.

"Dolly Fairchild. She's decided to move up the opening of her new store to this afternoon."

Simon swiveled back around. "The Cookie Jar?" he asked enthusiastically.

"The Cookie Jar?" I repeated less enthusiastically. I walked back to my desk, leaned back in my chair, and propped my feet up. Don't get me wrong. I loved desserts. However, I also loved being able to squeeze into my clothes every morning. With what Hayden was paying me, I didn't have a lot of money to buy a new wardrobe every few months. Besides, I live in Florida where it is bathing suit weather all year round. After several years of my life yo-yo dieting, the last thing I wanted to do was put on the weight I had taken off.

"That's the name," Hayden said. "Dolly's Cookie Jar and Sweets Emporium. It's a bakery. Pies, cakes, cookies, and candies. Everything good and sweet in the world."

Simon reached into his desk drawer. A few seconds later, he held a colorful brochure up. "But it wasn't supposed to open for another week."

Hayden shrugged. "She's decided to take advantage of the Valentine's Day holiday, and rush the opening. It's opening today at noon." He looked down at me and smiled. "Sample one of everything."

I felt the button of my beige Capris dig into my stomach.

"Why does she get to go?" Simon whined. "I've been looking forward to this for months. I love Miss Dolly's desserts." He looked over at me. "You know, I worked for her at her catering business during high school. It was because of her influence that I sincerely considered switching from journalism school to cooking school my first year of college."

My feet slid off the desk with a thump. "What?"

Hayden shook his head. "No."

"He wanted to be a baker?" I pointed to the kid. "Hayden, there's your food columnist. He actually enjoys this kind of thing."

"I don't care. Dolly Fairchild has personally asked for your attendance. Why, I have no idea." He glanced back at the letters and frowned. "Surely, she's read your column."

"I know her," I said. "She's my mom's best friend."

Hayden looked over at me with one dark eyebrow raised. "Really?"

"I was also good friends with her children growing up. I practically lived at her house. I blame her for my awkward teenage years. She kept me plump and well-fed."

"Is that good?" Hayden asked.

"It's not horrible." I relaxed a bit. At least I had no worry of being poisoned by Dolly.

"Excellent!" He glanced down at his watch as he headed to his office. "You'd better get a move on."

I waited until Hayden disappeared into his office before glancing over at Simon. "Let's go, Simon."

Simon made a face. "What?"

I clapped my hands together. "Come on now. Grab your camera. We're spending the day at the Cookie Jar."

CHAPTER TWO

I SHUT THE door to my blue convertible, stepped out onto the cobble stone sidewalk in front of our town's outdoor shopping mall and looked beyond the mall's giant wrought iron archway and toward the colorful old-fashioned Parisian storefronts that lay beyond. The only difference between our shops and the ones found in Paris were the colors chosen by the town. Our town elders, in their infinite wisdom, had decided to declare by ordinance that absolutely no normal neutral colors would be allowed. Only bright neon colors would do. I sometimes wondered if they wanted to make sure that our town was clearly visible from space.

I slipped on my sunglasses, a requisite part of the uniform in Florida, which also consisted of flip-flops, shorts, tank tops, and copious amounts of sunscreen and surveyed the long broad walkway in front of me, looking for any sign of Dolly's store. It didn't take long to find it. Five or six shops away from the south side entrance, I spotted a neon pink store front with numerous pink and green balloons and a large red carpet just screaming, GRAND OPENING.

Simon slammed the door and slung his camera bag over his shoulder. "Hayden's going to be mad."

"Nonsense. He'll be pleased that you showed initiative," I said, leading him to the bright pink store. Once in front of the store, my eyes naturally drifted up toward the giant, neon lime-green *Miss Dolly's Cookie Jar and Sweets Emporium* sign hanging above the French doors. "I guess this is it." I pushed open the white picket gate, passed the outdoor seating area and glanced into one of the large picturesque windows where every dessert imaginable was on display.

Simon jostled my arm as he rushed by me to get a better look. He stopped a few inches from the window and gazed at the desserts with the intensity of a starving man. "Just how much can we charge to our expense account?"

"Down boy," I said. "Why don't you take a picture?"

Simon reluctantly backed away from the window. He dropped his camera case on the nearest table, opened it and pulled out the camera while keeping his eyes focused on the goodies in the display window. Once the camera was in his hands, he lifted it up and pointed it toward the storefront.

"Good! Let's take another one. It usually works better if you take the lens cover off."

Simon glanced down at the camera as Dolly Fairchild, in a tight pink lace dress with a frilly apron, bustled out of the store, frantically waving both of her hands. "Wait! Wait! We're not completely set up yet." She reached up and clamped a hand on the top of her head, as wind swept through, tousling her strawberry blonde curls. She roughly pushed her hair away from her face as a big smile lit up her face. "Well, Kitty Kat, is that you?" She ran forward and enveloped me in a big hug, shaking my body back and forth repeatedly, which was not helping my weakened stomach. Once I had been thoroughly shaken and stirred, she held me out at arm's length. "Look at you. You're all skin and bones." She grinned. "Oh, I'm about to change that."

"Is that a threat?" I asked with a laugh.

I whipped my head back, as Simon stuck his face between Dolly's face and mine. "Hi, Miss Dolly. Do you remember me?"

"Oh...yes, of course. Of course." Dolly glanced at me for help.

"Simon, when did you say you worked for Dolly?"

Dolly's smile widened. She let go of my arms and grabbed Simon in a bear hug. "Simon! It's so good to see you again," she said shaking his rail thin body like a rag doll. "I didn't know you were back from college already. Oh my, how time flies." She set him down and grabbed me by the hand. "You must come inside and see my new store." She wagged her finger in my face. "Now, no pictures just yet. We still have an hour until opening and I want everything to be perfect." She patted my hand. "Now, Kitty Kat, I don't want you to be upset, but I'm going to be upfront with you." She gave me a worried glance. "I've invited several newspapers in the area, but don't you worry, sweetie, I plan on giving you an exclusive interview."

Smiling, I quickly assured her that I understood.

Dolly brightened immediately. "Good. Now, you must try everything. I want to know what you think of my new store and baked goodies."

I snagged Simon's arm. "That's why I brought Simon. He has such a sweet tooth."

Dolly pushed open the French door, which set the little bell above the door to jingling. "Oh good, you'll both enjoy—" Her voice faltered as she looked toward the back of the shop. I craned my neck to see what had captured her attention, and saw nothing but an empty store with a dozen café tables and a large, old-fashioned display case filled with various assortments of candy and cookies.

I turned back to Dolly. She tilted her head to the side, as a slight frown marred her pretty features. I followed her gaze to a glass door just beyond the display case and saw Rich Fairchild, Dolly's husband, pacing back and forth in front of the door as he spoke into a cell phone. He looked angry. Furious actually. His normally handsome face was set in an ugly scowl.

Catching Dolly's eye through the glass door, he quickly ended his call and walked away from the door. "Hmm, I wonder what's gotten into him," she said more to herself than me. "Oh dear, I hope there isn't a problem." She pulled out a chair and shoved me into it. "I better go check on Rich. You two wait here." She started to go into the back, but paused. She glanced from me to the door a couple of times, before running to the display case and carelessly tossing an assortment of heart shaped cookies on a silver serving tray. Once she had filled the tray with as many cookies as she could, she dashed back over and placed it on the table in front of me. "Now, I want to see this tray cleaned by the time I get back, you hear?" She clucked her tongue. "Oh, look at you, Kitty Kat. You're wasting away."

I nodded. I wasn't doing any such thing, but it was a nice ego boost to hear anyway.

Dolly turned to Simon. "She was such a picky eater as a child. Hated everything. I finally figured out how to get her to eat." She smiled brightly. "Lard."

My mouth fell open. "What?"

Still smiling indulgently, she patted my cheek. "Lots and lots of lard. It was the only thing you seemed to like."

Well, that explains why I gained fifty pounds in one year. I dropped my sunglasses down on the table and watched slightly horrified, as Simon, with a cookie in each hand, stuffed his mouth. His eyes rolled back in his head. "This is the best stuff ever," he said. At least, I think that was what he said. It was hard to tell what he was saying considering his mouth was full of sugar cookies and frosting. "I went to beat sing and more," he added for good measure.

I frowned. *Um, probably not.* "What did you say?"

Simon took a second to swallow. "I want to eat everything in the store."

Beaming with pride, Dolly walked to the back door. She pointed to the display case and called out, "When you two are done, make sure to help yourself to a piece of red velvet cake. It's a new recipe. I want to know what you both think." She turned back around. "Oh, and Kitty Kat, I made your favorite, devil's food cake with cream cheese frosting. I added another layer of frosting, just the way you like it. Help yourself to a piece of that, as well," she said before disappearing into the back, a flutter of pink lace.

"Kitty Kat?" Simon asked with a raised eyebrow.

"Please, don't call me that."

"It's better than some of the names Beatrix calls me." He picked up another cookie, stopped, went pale, and threw himself to the floor, quickly disappearing underneath the pink and white tablecloth.

Now, in some of the other towns that I had worked in, and with any other co-worker, I might have taken that as a warning sign to drop to the floor as well. Since I was in Hatter's Cove and the most frightening thing around was all the calories lying on the tray in front of me, I decided the best course of action, was to prop my hand underneath my chin and ask, "Is there a problem?"

"Look outside," he whispered from underneath the table.

Curious, I glanced over my shoulder. Two men were standing at the door talking to one another. I recognized the older of the two as being Evan Quincy, the Gazette's former star reporter, and the town's current resident letch. From Gazette lore, Evan was the first to jump ship five months ago. He was also the one that encouraged the others to join him in the land of milk and honey at the Hatter's Cove Herald, where there was a corner office for everyone, and the ink and paper roamed free.

I watched in fascination as Evan glanced from his companion to his reflection in the window. He licked his forefinger and brought it up to his forehead, securing a lock of hair that had fallen from his pronounced widow's peak back into place. Sticking out his ruby red lips in a pout, he leered at his reflection for an uncomfortable amount of time, before suddenly turning to glare at the younger man in front of him.

Evan was considered, mostly by himself, to be a ladies man. I had only had a few interactions with him since returning home, and that was more than enough to learn that the only important things in Evan's life were himself, his reputation, and fashion. Or what he considered fashion. His usual attire, whether at work or at play, normally consisted of a Hawaiian shirt, long shorts, sandals, and an ample amount of gold chains around his neck. Today was no different. He was decked out in an electric blue Hawaiian shirt with purple palm trees, lavender walking shorts, and four or five gold chains. If it weren't for the dark tan, the shirt, shorts and white sandals, he would be the spitting image of Count Dracula. As it was, he looked like an aging, burnt sienna, Eddie Munster on vacation.

Feeling the top of Simon's head brush against my calf, I moved my leg to the side to give him more room to cower before tapping on the tabletop with my knuckles. "I know you consider the Herald people to be traitors, but don't you think this is a bit extreme."

"No, I'm not hiding from Evan," Simon said from beneath the table. "I'm hiding from Benny."

I glanced back to the two men. The other man, a paper-thin young man with bright red hair, was holding up his hands as though he was being robbed and shaking his head. He was dressed only slightly worse than Evan was, with a green tuxedo and matching top hat. I glanced down at my attire, wondering if I was properly dressed for this event. "Who's Benny?" I asked, glancing back toward the window.

"He's a creep," Simon answered. "We used to work together for Miss Dolly."

"That doesn't explain why you're hiding from him."

Simon stuck his head out from underneath the table. "He threatened to kill me if he ever saw me again."

I was about to ask why, when Benny's back suddenly landed against the French door with a loud thud. Being a concerned citizen, I immediately reached for the camera Simon had laid on the table and began snapping pictures. Unfortunately, whatever had happened between Evan and Benny was over.

Benny threw open the door and raced to the back of the store, while Evan stood at the entrance eyeing me, or rather the camera in my hand. I smiled and waved, as Simon crawled back out from underneath the table. Evan didn't return my greeting. Shaking his head, he reached into his pocket, pulled out his phone and walked away from the store.

"I didn't know Benny still worked for Miss Dolly," Simon said with a worried look. "I thought he was working at the courthouse."

Ah, so that explained the panicked look he threw my way when Hayden assigned him to the courthouse an hour ago. "Why does he want to kill you?" I asked, turning back around and facing him.

"The last summer I worked for Miss Dolly at her catering company, I discovered that someone was stealing money and supplies. I figured it was probably Benny, and told her what I thought. She said she couldn't fire anyone without solid proof. Unfortunately, Benny overheard us talking and got real mad. I've been avoiding him ever since."

I glanced back over my shoulder as the bells above the front door jingled, and Evan strolled up to our table. "My man, Simon Says," he said pounding Simon on the back, causing the younger man to wince. After he had beaten the poor boy sufficiently enough, Evan scooped up a cookie. "How've you been, Simon Says?"

"My name is not Simon Says," the said mentioned Simon Says whined in exasperation. "It's Simon Sayors. Say it with me. S-a-y-o-r-s."

Evan slowly swallowed the rest of the cookie he had shoved in his mouth and began licking his fingers. "I'm sorry. You're right." He patted Simon on the shoulder. "Hey, how about Simple Simon? Come to visit the pie man or the woman in this case." He shoved another cookie into his mouth. As soon as he finished chewing, he leaned over the table. "So, did you tell Kat about that *big* story you were working on right before she joined the Gazette?" Giggling like an idiot, he turned to me. "Simple Simon here was convinced the police chief was taking bribes, so he set up a sting." He began laughing harder. "Hayden had to bail Edward R. Murrow here out of jail, for guess what? Bribery."

Simon flushed as he looked down at the table. He half-heartedly brought a cherub shaped cookie up to his mouth, snapping its head clear off with one bite.

While Simon ate away at the little cherub, the injustice of it all ate away at me. Being older and wiser, I calmly and with extreme politeness, explained to Evan that ours is a noble profession, and that we should treat each other as equals and with the utmost respect.

"I am not a loser," Evan responded. "I happen to be doing quite well at the Herald," he said, before rambling on about the benefits of working at the Herald over the third world conditions at the Gazette.

"Yeah, yeah, I'm sure the hallways are lined with gold," I said waving his sales pitch aside. "What was with you and Benny Boy over there?"

Evan ignored the question. "I even have my own personal Keurig."

"Congratulations." I crossed my arms. "What's such an important guy like you doing covering a store opening?"

Evan's smug look faltered as he struggled to come up with a reason.

"Uh huh," I said. "Now, about Benny—"

Unfortunately, Dolly came out of the back door at that moment carrying a tray loaded with cookies. She took one look at Evan and scowled. *Who could blame her?* I thought, not the least bit surprised that Evan Quincy could make even sweet-natured Dolly Fairchild angry.

My eyes drifted above her head as Benny came into view. He stood just behind her, and I noticed Benny's face wore the exact same expression as Dolly's, only it was directed in equal parts at Evan and Simon.

"Oh no, dear me, we're not open yet," Dolly said with forced politeness. "You must leave, Mr. Quincy." She dropped the tray on the nearest counter and shooed Evan out. I watched in amusement as he moaned and complained his way out the door.

Simon looked up. "I can't stand that guy." He dropped the remnants of the cherub back on the tray and stared morosely at the tablecloth. "I hate my name."

Feeling sorry for the kid, I leaned forward. "Do you know what my name is, Simon?"

"Of course, it's Kat Archer."

"My full name is Kitty Katherine Archer."

Simon's face twisted in a grimace as he tilted his head, which I was sorry to admit, was the normal reaction whenever I told anyone my name. "But, isn't Kitty short for Katherine?"

"Yes, yes it is. Do you know why my parents named me Kitty Katherine?"

Simon shook his head.

"So my mother could call me Kitty Kat. That's it. That's the only reason. They're very cruel people. See, Mom's cat had just died before I was born, so I got stuck with Kitty Kat. It could have been worse. I could have been Mrs. Wiggles."

Simon's lips curled up as he reached for another cookie.

"Simon, have you ever heard of a Pulitzer prize winner with the name of Kitty Kat?" At a shake of his head, I said, "No, of course not. Nor has there been a network anchor, a Supreme Court justice, or a president that was named Kitty Kat. However, that was my name, until I was fifteen years old, and I made my parents swear never to call me that again. For a glorious seven years of my life, I was simply known as Kat or Katherine. Then at my first job after college, I made the mistake of telling someone what my name was. Huge mistake. After that, I was back to being called Kitty Kat."

"How awful," he said over another mouthful of cookie. Or at least that's what I thought he said. It came out sounding more like, "Ough oulul," but I pressed on.

"Yes, it was awful, but you know, I got used to it because I realized something important. I was now one of them." I leaned forward and adopted my best teaching voice. "I was part of the team. By calling me Kitty Kat, they were letting me into their inner circle. I was accepted."

"Really?"

Despite lying through my teeth, I nodded and patted his hand.

"Oh, I didn't think of that. So when Evan calls me Simon Says, it's sort of a badge of honor?"

I shrugged. Sounded good to me. "Sure."

Simon smiled. "That makes me feel better. Thanks, Kitty Kat."

Trying and failing to keep from grimacing, I patted his hand. "Let's stick with Kat."

CHAPTER THREE

I WAS GOING to be sick. I had tried the fudge, the cake, the candy, and the cookies. Just when I thought I couldn't take it anymore, Dolly thrust a spoonful of some pink concoction down my throat.

"Isn't it yummy?" she asked. "I call it Cotton Candy Rush. Don't you just love it?"

I squeaked out a yes as my stomach flip-flopped. Suddenly, Mack's All You Can Eat Crab Shack was becoming the highlight of my week. I shook my head as sugar overload set in, and all the colors in the store began to dance before my eyes. I reached for my purse. "Well, it's been fun, Dolly."

"Oh, hang on just a second. I have something for you," she called out as she weaved through the crowd. I glanced back at my watch. With any luck, I'd be out of here and back at the Gazette in an hour or so. Seconds later, Dolly reappeared at my side holding a pink and green striped bag in her hands. "I made this especially for you. It's a new recipe. Chocolate Chip Cookie Surprise. The surprise is in the filling. It's made of chocolate and raspberry with just a hint of espresso. I know how much you love raspberry."

I didn't. My sister did, but I nodded politely anyway.

"Oh, I can't wait to read your article!" Dolly gave me a quick hug. "Your mother and I will be reading it together."

I narrowed my eyes. *I recognized a threat when I heard one.* "Where is my mother? I figured she would be here to support you."

"She had another commitment at the country club, but we're going to get together real soon." How Dolly could make something so innocent sound so frightening was a testament to her years around my mother. She patted my arm. "Real soon."

Like a true blackmail victim, I nodded my understanding. *Write a great review or else.* She nodded right back at me before moving on to her next victim, one of the anchors from the five o'clock news.

I almost rebelled, my natural inclination to stubbornness started to kick in, but the truth of the matter was that Dolly knew her way around the kitchen. In the years I had been gone, Dolly had developed a reputation as a first class baker and chef in Hatter's Cove. And as a testament to her skills, the Cookie Jar was packed to the brim with excited customers. I watched as Benny, still dressed in his lime green tuxedo with bright pink waistcoat, green top hat, and red muttonchops to match his red hair, worked his way around the room carrying a serving tray full of samples.

"I can't believe *she's* here," Simon said softly with a touch of awe from just behind me.

The reporter in me immediately piped up. "What? Who? Where?"

Simon pointed to a pretty, petite, young woman with short, sun-kissed, light brown hair, in a purple sundress and purple leather jacket standing in line. She took a cookie from Benny's tray and nibbled at its edge, while Benny whispered in her ear. "That's Tiffany Wallace," Simon said, "I figured she would have moved away after she was released."

"Released?"

"She's a convicted murderer. Evan covered her trial for the Gazette."

"Really? Who did she kill?"

"Her dad. She killed him six years ago on her eighteenth birthday."

I looked at him in surprise. "Six years ago. How is she out after only six years?"

Simon looked over his shoulder before lowering his head to mine and whispered, "The prosecutor knocked down the charge from murder to manslaughter. Evan said that there was no way it was manslaughter. It was premeditated murder." He shrugged. "In any event, she pled guilty to manslaughter, and the judge sentenced her as a youthful offender. He gave her the maximum six years in a state correctional-rehabilitation program. It was a pretty big scandal at the time. Evan was convinced she paid the judge and prosecutor off to get the reduced charge. She was released about a month ago." He shook his head. "Sad. We went to school together. She was way out of my league though."

"Why did she kill her dad?"

"Because of Benny. Can you believe it? She used to date Benny Yates." He grimaced. "James Wallace hated him. Most people hate Benny. Anyway, Benny asked her to marry him and Mr. Wallace flipped out. He told her that he would cut her off without a dime if she even thought about marrying the creep."

"So that's James Wallace's daughter. My mother told me all about her. She poisoned him with strychnine, didn't she?"

"Yeah. Do you see that woman over there?" He pointed to the corner of the room, and the stunningly beautiful woman with long blonde hair sneering at the cookie she held between one long finger and thumb. She turned it upside down as though inspecting it for a hair before tossing it into the garbage can next to her. "That's Vivian Wallace. You've probably heard of her. She was the runner up in the Miss Florida pageant thirty years ago. She's Tiffany's step-mom."

I had a vague memory of my mother describing Vivian's wedding to me over the phone while I was away in college. It apparently was quite the to-do. "I know her. My mother, Vivian, and Dolly, grew up together. They all had been close friends since kindergarten."

"Really? I didn't think Dolly and Vivian were friends. Vivian seems to hate her, though I don't know why."

"Vivian and Dolly went into the catering business with one another fifteen years ago. Turned out to be a big mistake. Vivian made a mess of the finances and when the business went under, so did their friendship. They split ways and started their own catering companies."

"Vivian Wallace is a baker?" he asked in surprise.

"Well, actually no. That was the problem. Dolly was the one with the talent. Her business thrived while Vivian's died a slow and painful death. She lost all her money and declared bankruptcy a few years later. She made up for the shortfall however, by marrying the wealthiest man in town."

"Oh," Simon said, seemingly uninterested by that piece of gossip. "Well, I think it's time to make my move."

Wondering what Simon was talking about, I glanced over my shoulder and watched as he picked the glass of Cotton Candy Rush Dolly had left for me and downed it in one shot. Taking a deep breath, he slammed it down on the table before turning his bright brown eyes toward Tiffany Wallace. "I'm going to go say hi to Tiffany."

I was about to ask if that was a good idea, but noticing that Benny had moved on and was nowhere near Tiffany, I decided to let him go. *Who knows, maybe the kid could get a story from the young woman about her father's murder.* Armed with the Cookie Jar's version of liquid courage, Simon pushed himself away from the table and strolled toward Tiffany, while I turned my attention back to her stepmother, Vivian.

While I had been chatting with Simon, Dolly must have finally noticed Vivian standing near the display case. The two women glared at each other from across the store. *With any luck, the two might liven up this grand opening,* I thought, as I leaned back in my chair. Disappointment quickly set in, however, as Dolly purposely weaved around the crowd of customers, taking care to keep as wide a berth as possible from her former friend. Rich Fairchild, however, didn't seem to have the same aversion. He sauntered past Vivian without saying a word. He didn't even look her way as he passed. Nor did he react when her hand reached out and placed a blue colored note in his fingers, which he promptly slipped into his pocket.

Rich Fairchild and Vivian Wallace? My heart constricted in my chest as I thought about Dolly. I liked Dolly. She was one of my mother's oldest friends and had always been kind to me. I didn't like seeing her hurt. *Perhaps I was wrong though.* I looked back at Vivian's face. A half smile played around her lips, as she watched Rich walk away and I knew that I wasn't wrong. There was definitely something going on between them. Rich was quite a bit younger than either woman, and I could see what they both saw in him with his light tousled blond hair, athletic build, and chiseled good looks. *Poor Dolly,* I thought, as I watched Rich pass by the giant display case filled with cookies.

I was so focused on Rich Fairchild that it came as quite the surprise when Simon went flying into the display case, sending cookies of every shape and color imaginable, soaring into the air. To my credit, I recovered quickly however, and reached for the camera.

* * *

"The St. Valentine's Day Cookie Massacre?" Hayden asked. "That's your headline? Didn't we talk about toning down your articles?" He picked up the bubblegum pink and green striped cookie bag that Dolly had given me, and eyed the cookies within suspiciously. "Just how bad were the cookies?"

"This has nothing to do with the cookies," I said as my fingers flew over the keyboard. "The headline accurately reflects what happened. There were cookie crumbs everywhere." I watched as he examined the cookie carefully, before dropping it back into the bag. "No, really, I'm sure they're fine. They're probably delicious." I felt his hand grip the back of my chair as he bent over and read the screen. My stomach gave an involuntary flutter as he leaned closer and his head neared mine.

I suddenly missed my old editor in Miami. *I never had these feelings around old Bulldog Barnes,* named such because of his looks, and his temperament. I glanced at Hayden. There was nothing bulldog like about Hayden, with his soft sea-green eyes, strong jaw, and lean body. I turned my eyes back to the computer screen with a sigh. Office romances never work, and I sincerely wished that I didn't have to keep reminding myself of that whenever Hayden was near.

He dropped the cookie bag back onto my desk. "Bang? Crash?" He reached forward and hit the down arrow on the keyboard. "The wrought iron table fell to the floor with an ear shattering BANG? Bang? There is no reason for 'bang' to be in your article."

"Aren't you always telling me to be more descriptive?"

"About the food." He waved his hand at the computer screen. "This reads like an old Batman comic book."

"I felt like I was in a comic book. You should have seen the way Benny was dressed." I tilted my head to the side. "You know, now that I think about it, he kind of looked like the Riddler."

"What happened there?" Hayden leaned forward once again and tapped at the down arrow. His eyes widened in surprise. "Wait," he said, "Simon? Simon got into a fight with Benny Yates at the grand opening? Over Tiffany Wallace?"

As if hearing his name, Simon shuffled through the door. He held a bunch of tissues up to his nose.

"Surely, it's stopped bleeding by now," I said.

Simon tilted his head back. "I sneezed and it started again."

Hayden glared at Simon. "I sent you there to cover the news; not become it." He frowned. "Wait a second. I didn't send you at all. Why were you there?"

Simon kept his head tilted back as he pointed an accusatory finger at me. "She made me go."

Hayden took a breath and turned to me. "Where were you when all of this went down?"

I held up the camera. "Taking pictures. I have some great shots." I sank back in my chair at his less than pleased look. "Simon wanted to go. Hey, I didn't know it would turn into a three ring circus. You should have seen Simon and Benny go at it, Hayden. At one point Benny was lobbing cookies at people's heads just to keep them away."

"Yeah, I'm sure it was the fight of the century," Hayden said with a smirk. "Where is Benny Yates now?"

Simon gently pressed his fingers to the bridge of his nose. "The coward took off before the police got there."

"There's a warrant out for him right now," I added. I glanced over at Simon, as he began hastily removing the tissues from his nose and sitting up straighter.

I looked over toward the door. Sure enough, Rosie was here. She did a double take at Simon's appearance. "Oh, sweetie, are your allergies acting up again?"

Simon shook his head, wincing slightly.

Beatrix followed Rosie into the room. She took one look at Simon and rolled her eyes. "What happened?" Her ruby red lips tilted up in a nasty imitation of a smile. "Did you trip and fall on your face again?"

I quickly caught Rosie and Beatrix up to date, pleased when Rosie looked at Simon with renewed interest. Simon threw me a grateful look. "Simon was amazing." Amazingly bad, but they didn't need to know that part. He went down at the first punch, started wheezing, and immediately rolled into a protective ball. "He could have been a pro-fighter." *Oops, went too far,* I thought, as Hayden and Beatrix shared a disbelieving look. "You should have seen Benny Yates," I quickly added. "After it was all over, they had to carry him out of the store. I think his nose was broken." Granted, most of the damage to Benny came from a heavy ceramic cake stand falling onto his head, but I felt that wasn't really necessary to point out.

Simon groaned. "My nose won't stop throbbing."

Hayden closed his eyes. "Simon, go home."

"I'm dizzy," Simon said, as he began to wheeze.

Rosie held out her hand. "Come on, Simon. I'll drive you to your place."

Hayden shook his head. "I need your article on that surfing event, Rosie. Beatrix can take him home."

Beatrix's brown eyes widened. "Bu—but, I just got here."

"And you're also the only one not busy right now," Hayden pointed out calmly.

Everyone froze. Even Simon's wheezing quieted as we waited for Beatrix's reaction. She wasn't known as the Queen Bee for nothing.

To my surprise, Beatrix simply said, "As you wish. Let's go, Simon."

Simon reluctantly rose to his feet.

"Hey, Simon, here, take these with you." I picked up the pink and green striped gift bag of cookies and tossed them at Simon. He fumbled the bag, but Rosie caught them just before they hit the ground and pressed it into his hands.

Simon turned worried, already blackened eyes toward his employer. "Are you firing me?"

"No, I'm not," Hayden said. "It wasn't your fault."

Beatrix rolled her eyes before dragging Simon out of the room.

As soon as the door closed behind Simon and Beatrix, Hayden turned on me. "It was your fault."

Rosie threw me an amused look before powering up her computer.

"How is it my fault?" I asked.

"Number one, he shouldn't have been there," Hayden said. "It was your assignment."

"I didn't know a brawl would break out."

"Number two, you are the experienced one. You should have gotten him out of there when you realized there might be trouble." Hayden began to pace. "You know, when I hired you, I didn't really believe the rumors about you."

"What rumors?"

"That trouble follows you wherever you go and that you sometimes are the one that creates the trouble. Just in case, I decided to put you in the life section. I stupidly thought that nothing's going to happen there. Now, Simon is getting into fights and you're receiving death threats. Do you know that in the hundred years this paper has been in existence, none of our reporters have ever received death threats?"

"Then, obviously you all have been doing something wrong," I pointed out with a smile.

Rosie giggled.

Hayden didn't seem as amused. "I cannot believe—"

I held up my hand, stopping him in mid-tirade, and reached for the ringing phone on my desk. *Saved by the bell.* "Hel—"

"Is this Kat? I mean, Katherine Archer," a male voice said in a rush, before I could finish spitting out my greeting. "You don't know me, but I saw you at the Cookie Jar today. I need to talk to you urgently."

"Yeah, what about?"

The voice dropped to a whisper. "I can't talk on the phone. Someone might overhear. It's a big story. I'm going to right a wrong that was done. Just meet me behind the Cookie Jar at eleven-thirty tonight. Come alone. If I see anyone else, I'll go to one of the Herald's reporters and tell them what I know. I might just do that anyway. I have something big. Real big."

"Uh huh, and that would be what?" Silence greeted my perfectly valid question. "Could I at least get your name?" Still more silence. I hung up and tapped my nails against the phone. Could be a crank, but then again...

"What was that about?" Hayden asked.

"I think I just got a date for Valentine's Day."

* * *

I turned off the engine to my car and looked around. Despite the darkness and the fact the majority of shops were now closed, people were still milling about, going to and from the movie theater at the end of the street.

I leaned over the back of my seat and reached for a pair of sneakers. I was pretty sure my mysterious caller was nothing more than a crank, but I wanted to be prepared to run just in case my secret admirer turned out to be dangerous. Since flip-flops were not proper running gear, I tossed them into the backseat of my car and slipped on a pair of tennis shoes, before leaning over and opening the glove compartment.

A movement to my right caught my eye. I rose up and looked over at the other parked cars. Evan Quincy was hurrying away from the shops. His head swiveled from right to left as he looked from shop to shop, obviously searching for something. Catching my eye, he stopped and stared for a second, before turning back around and rushing away.

I grabbed a flashlight from the glove compartment and slid out of my car. Checking to make sure the flashlight still worked, I passed by the pretty well lit storefronts, into the not so pretty, or well-lit alleyway behind the stores. I reached one hand into my purse and grabbed hold of the can of mace I kept close by—just in case.

"One, two, three," I counted quietly as I passed by each back door. I stopped at number six. This had to be the door to the Cookie Jar. The color pink spilled out of the dumpster. Pink ribbon, pink boxes, pink and red Valentine decorations, and remnants of pink and green napkins were strewn across the alleyway, the wind having tossed them to and fro since the grand opening several hours before. Even if I hadn't noticed the profuse amount of pink littering the alley, the overwhelming smell of sugar would have definitely clued me into my location.

I looked down both ends of the alleyway. Other than a white cat wandering around the dumpster near the burger joint, the place was empty. I glanced at my watch. Eleven-thirty on the dot. I hate it when my sources are late. How hard is it to show up on time, especially when you ask a lady to meet in such a charming location.

The cat jumped onto the fence that ran along the back of the alleyway. It howled, calling to its little kitty friends. Almost immediately, another howl issued from the back of the fence. In a few seconds, I was being serenaded by a cacophony of kitty howls and screeches.

"Wonderful. Just wonderful." I leaned back against the fence. "Ten minutes. That's all I'm giving him," I said to a calico cat that appeared just above my head on the fence. The poor calico looked like it had seen better days. One ear had been nicked and one eye was missing. My companion paid me little attention, as he or she bounded over my head and ran to the dumpster. Being a fan of westerns and of a father who loved John Wayne, I immediately christened the cat, Rooster.

I watched as the furry little hunter chased something small from behind the dumpster to a row of small metal garbage cans near the Cookie Jar's back door. Another cat quickly joined Rooster, and from the sound of it, Rooster, was none too pleased to have company. *Who could blame him? I rarely liked company when I was chasing something down either.* I jumped back as Rooster and the other cat bounded out from behind the garbage can, knocking them over with a loud bang in the process.

After chasing off the competition, Rooster strolled up near me. He dropped a red furry thing at my feet, before promptly chasing after another cat that appeared next to the dumpster.

"Thanks." I glanced down at the disgusting thing, wondering how my life had come to this, when I realized the red furry thing at my feet was man-made. I pushed my hair behind my ears and leaned over. It was a mutton-chop. *Definitely part of Benny's costume.* I kicked it to the side and shook my head. *I can't believe I'm standing in a dark alleyway waiting for a stranger to show up on Valentine's Day. And the worst part about it is that I think I've been stood up.*

After ten minutes had passed without one sign of another human being, I decided that my night could be better spent watching cats on the internet from the safety of my own living room. I was just about to push myself away from the fence when my phone rang. *This better be my secret valentine,* I thought as I answered the phone.

"Is your hand broken? Why haven't you called me?" Hayden asked on the other end of the line.

"Why do you sound like my mother?" I looked down as Rooster weaved around my ankles. I bent down and petted the cat, who began to purr.

"I thought we agreed that you would keep me apprised of what was going on. Now, what's happening?"

"He's a no show." I gasped in surprise as a gray and white cat jumped down from the fence, and landed on a crate next to my feet. He gave me a baleful look, before hissing and making a swipe at my legs with his claws. "Hey, I was here first, buddy." The cat didn't care. He issued another hiss. Just then, Rooster leapt to my defense and chased the other cat away.

"Are you okay?" Hayden asked in a panic. "Who are you talking to?"

"No one. Just a cat."

"Oh, well, call it a night. Whoever it is probably isn't going to show anyway."

"Yeah, you're probably right," I said as I moved away from the fence. I had only taken a few steps, when I noticed something strange out of the corner of my eye. There were two feet sticking out from behind the row of metal garbage cans that Rooster and the other cat had knocked over. "Um, Hayden, I'll call you right back." I slipped my phone back in my purse, and I pointed my flashlight toward the legs, as I carefully closed the distance between me and whoever had decided to take a nap behind the store.

Lime green pants were the first thing I noticed. I took a step closer and ran the light up the legs, over the bright pink waistcoat, onto a ghastly pale hand which was clutching a pink and green striped bag and then up even further into the dead blue eyes of Benny Yates.

CHAPTER FOUR

"YATES," ONE OF the many uniformed officers milling about said into the radio attached to his shoulder. "Benedict Henry Yates. Male. Caucasian. Red hair. Blue eyes. Six-four. One hundred and seventy-five pounds. Twenty-four years old." He paused long enough to shoo two cats away from Benny and the other officers leaning over Benny's body. Cats being cats, however, immediately turned in the opposite direction and toward the body.

"Would someone get these cats out of here?" one of the officers shouted. He threw out his arm to ward off one curious cat.

Quickly scribbling down Benny's full name, I looked up in disappointment, as the officer I was eavesdropping on took off after the cats.

"Ma'am, why did you want to meet the deceased back here?" The young uniformed cop, who was standing in front of me, said once again with a decidedly strained voice.

I glanced back at him with an irritated shake of my head, as I explained once again that I didn't know who I was meeting and that I had already been questioned by another officer shortly after they had arrived at the scene. I didn't bother mentioning that the same officer had also ushered me to the end of the alley with an order to stay put. It had taken awhile, but I had slowly inched my way toward the Cookie Jar's back door and was finally close enough to overhear what was being said. Unfortunately, one of the police department's finest noticed, and decided to take that moment to try to question me once again.

I stood up on my tiptoes and craned my head to the side, just in time to see Clay Waltrip, Hatter's Cove's chief of police lean over the dead body and shake his head. "No, this doesn't look right. Look at his mouth."

"Ma'am, did you know the deceased?" Officer Davis said, stepping in front of me once again and cutting off my view of the body.

I resisted the urge to shush the youngster. I looked at him again, wondering just how old he was. He had to still be in his teens. Surely, he was too young to be a police officer. "You are over eighteen, aren't you?" I asked as I took another step closer to the body. I froze in horror. *Had I become so old that I was noticing how young people in authority now looked to me? I was only thirty-three. That wasn't old. Was it?*

Officer Davis earnestly nodded his head. "Yes ma'am, I'm twenty-nine."

Momentarily distracted, I swung my eyes back to the officer. "Do you take any sort of special vitamins?"

He shook his head. "Just regular exercise, healthy eating, and plenty of sleep."

Well, that lets me out. Seeing, as I didn't need to hear anymore of such nonsense, I held up my hand and refocused my attention on the chief of police, who took that moment to glance up in my direction. "What is she doing here?"

I smiled slightly. *You would think that at some time, I would get tired of my mere presence being a source of annoyance to others, but you'd be wrong.* "The press has every right to be here."

Waltrip stood up and planted his hands on his hips. He indicated the end of the alley with a jerk of his chin. "The press can wait back there."

I felt Officer Davis grab my upper arm.

Waltrip narrowed his eyes. "Wait a second. I thought you just did those lifestyle bits. What are you doing here at this time of night?"

I dug in my heels and leaned away from Officer Davis. "I'm not just the press in this case. I'm a witness."

Waltrip smacked his lips. He leaned his head to the side as he looked over my shoulder. "About time you showed up, Casey. First day on the job and you're late."

"Oh, dear God, no," a deep male voice said from behind me.

Recognizing the voice, I pivoted around on my heel. Luke Casey, all muscular six feet two inches of him, stood behind me. My breath caught in my throat. It usually did when I saw him. He was the very picture of tall, dark and handsome with dark blue eyes and thick, black hair. He hadn't changed much since I had last seen him more than four months ago in Miami. He was still the best-looking detective I had ever met. Frowning, I tilted my head to the side as I looked him over. Something was different about him though. His hair was longer than I remembered. He seemed a bit paler and thinner, too.

A look of exasperation crossed his handsome face. "Are you following me?"

Whatever friendly greeting I was about to give him, quickly fled out of my mind. To say that Luke and I had a bit of an antagonistic history with one another, would be putting it mildly. Normally, the police and press have a symbiotic relationship with one another. Some officers respected that relationship, while others didn't. Luke was one of those that had difficulty with that philosophy. He had developed a natural distrust of reporters after being burned a few times by some of my more zealous co-workers, but by the time I left Miami, I thought we had come to an uneasy truce built on mutual respect, and dare I say, a grudging friendship. "Following you? I hate to burst your bubble, but you'd be the last man I'd follow. Aren't you just a bit out of your jurisdiction? Miami's that way," I said pointing to my left.

Officer Davis leaned closer. "That way's the gulf."

"Thank you," I said, before changing direction and pointing my finger in the opposite direction. "Go home."

Luke placed his hands on his hips. "I am home. I just moved here."

"Oh, well," I said feeling a bit smug, "I moved here three months ago. So, if anyone is following anyone, it is you following me."

Luke smirked. "Believe me, if I knew you were here, I would have made sure not to come within a hundred miles from here."

"Really, detective?" I glanced down at my legs. Rooster hadn't left my side since the police and ambulance had arrived, and was now kneading my pants. I slipped my notebook into my purse, bent down, and picked Rooster up before turning back to Luke. "You didn't know I moved here?"

"I've got news for you. As soon as you are out of my sight, I try to forget all about you."

I pressed my hand to my chest. "You're breaking my heart."

Chief Waltrip pushed his way past Officer Davis. "I hate to interrupt this little reunion, but we have work to do." He turned and stared down at me. "All right, you're the one who found the body, is that correct?"

"Yes." I shifted Rooster to my right side, as I reached into the purse slung across my body and brought out my notebook once again. Realizing I wasn't going to be able to write and hold the cat at the same time, I thrust the animal into Luke's hands.

He gave me a pained look before shaking his head in disbelief.

I ignored him and flipped the book to an empty page. "Okay, have you been able to determine what he died of yet?" When my question was met with silence, I pressed on with a few more. "Any signs of foul play?"

Waltrip's bushy grey eyebrows drew together. "We won't know how he died until the coroner's report. Now, how do you know the victim?"

"Victim? So, you do think he was murdered."

Waltrip's frown deepened. "No."

"No? What, do you think a healthy twenty-four year old just decided to take a nap behind the garbage cans?" I tapped my pen against my mouth. "Drugs perhaps?"

Waltrip's eyes widened. "Drugs? Is that why you two were here in the alley?"

It was my turn to frown. "What? No, of course not. Then again, I don't really know why we were here. Did he have a history of drug arrests? Heroin? Cocaine?"

Waltrip glanced back at Benny's body. "Hmm. Heroin? You don't say?"

Luke rubbed a hand across his eyes and groaned.

I spared him a passing glance before turning back to the chief. "Did you see any needle tracks?"

Glancing back at me, Waltrip planted his hands on his hips and leaned forward. "Needle tracks?"

"Can I get you on tape?" I reached into my purse, lifted my cell phone out, and hit the record button just as Luke grabbed my wrist.

"No you may not," Luke said. "Put that thing away."

I sighed. I didn't think they would let me, but I figured it wouldn't hurt to ask. "Is this area known for its drug use?"

Waltrip eyed me warily. "Are you doing some sort of exposé?"

If Benny died of a drug overdose I just might. "Perhaps," I hedged. "So, you think Benny Yates was here on some type of drug deal gone wrong, or did he just overdose?"

"Well, we haven't been able to determine exactly how he died . . . an exposé on heroin, huh?" Waltrip rubbed a hand over his jaw. "Here in Hatter's Cove?"

Luke's eyes widened as he looked from his chief back to me. He shook his head. "Kat, how well do you know the deceased?"

"Not at all." I pointed to the body and the man leaning over him. "That's the coroner over there. He must have some idea about how he died. At the very least, he must have an educated guess. Can I talk to him?"

Luke raised his hands. He looked over at Chief Waltrip. "I have experience with her. Do you mind?" Before the Chief had a chance to object, Luke looked back at me, his dark blue eyes flashing as he pointed his finger at my chest. "I don't think you quite understand. You are a witness right now, not a reporter."

I raised my chin and gave him my most charming smile. "Listen, you know me, I'm open to a bit of quid pro quo."

Luke scowled. "No quid pro quo. You answer our questions. We don't answer yours."

I clicked the end of the pen and looked up at him expectantly, until he hung his head. "We don't know anything," he said through gritted teeth.

"Is that the official police statement on this matter, or is it a more general statement of fact?" I asked sweetly. "Also, can I quote you?"

"No, you may not quote me," Luke said with a small shake of his head. Suddenly remembering the cat in his hands, he thrust Rooster back in my arms. "We will have an official statement at a later date, but as of right now, we would like your cooperation."

"Hey, I'll cooperate," I said, trying to juggle Rooster and my notebook. Deciding that I had received about as much information as I could get, I quickly reiterated what led me to the Cookie Jar after closing hours.

"You said you received a call?" Luke asked. "From whom?"

"I have no idea, but I'm assuming it was Benny."

"What did he want to talk to you about?" Luke asked.

"Not a clue," I said.

"I thought you were here about some type of heroin exposé?" Waltrip asked.

Luke's lips pursed together. He turned to his boss and whispered, "I think there may have been some confusion. I'll explain later," he said before turning back to me. "What time did you receive the phone call?"

"About five."

Chief Waltrip opened a plastic bag which contained a cell phone. He thumbed through the phone for a few seconds before holding it up to me. "Is this your number?"

I nodded, while glancing at the other numbers listed on the screen. "Who do those other numbers belong to?"

Waltrip snapped the phone back.

"Speaking of phones," Luke said, holding out his hand. "I'd like to see yours."

I shook my head. "I told you, he called my office phone, not my cell."

"And I guess that you didn't take any pictures of the deceased while you were here waiting?"

I clutched my purse closer to my body. "Do you have a warrant, Detective?" I smiled as he dropped his hand. "I didn't think so."

Chief Waltrip looked like he swallowed a lemon. "All right, Ms. Archer, you may leave, but don't go far." I watched as he and Luke moved closer to the body. Officer Davis politely pointed to the end of the alleyway.

"All right, I'm going," I said when he gave me a little shove. I turned toward the end of the alley where a crowd of onlookers had gathered. One figure in particular caught my eye. Hayden stood at the edge of the crowd looking directly at me, a worried frown marring his handsome face. I smiled slightly and waved, pleased when his face relaxed, and he took a deep breath.

I was just about to continue walking toward Hayden, when I noticed Evan Quincy standing off to the side with his camera. I called out to Luke. "I may have something for you." When Luke and Waltrip walked back to me, I quickly described the altercation I witnessed earlier in the day between Benny and Evan.

"Evan Quincy, huh?" Waltrip smacked his lips. "That's strange. I thought Benny and him were close. Real close." He motioned for Luke to follow him. When I tried to tag along, he pointed toward the end of the alleyway. "Press stands back over there." He turned back around, nearly tripping over a cat in the process. "Would someone get these cats out of here," he bellowed at the top of his lungs. "They're contaminating the crime scene."

"Thank you for keeping in touch," Hayden said, holding up his phone as I approached. "I almost had a heart attack when I saw the cops and the ambulance."

I winced. "Sorry, I was a little distracted."

Hayden looked down at the cat I was carrying. He scratched Rooster's chin. "Friend of yours?"

"I think he's adopted me. I wish I could take him home, but unfortunately, my apartment doesn't allow pets."

I lifted Rooster up and looked at him in the eye. "It wouldn't be fair to him anyway. I'm always at the office."

"I know," Hayden said, "you have no life."

"Speak for yourself. You're always at work, too."

"That's how I know you have no life." Hayden ran his hand down Rooster's back. "We can keep him at the office."

"Really?"

"He can take care of our rat problem." He glanced toward the alley. "What happened?"

"We have a rat problem?"

Hayden gestured to the police officers standing in the alley. "Yes, now what happened back there?"

I was about to explain, when I saw Evan Quincy barreling his way through the throng of people toward us. "What happened?" Evan asked as soon as he reached my side.

"Got me." I glanced down at his lavender shorts. Dirt and mud covered the fabric and one seam was ripped. "The police aren't talking."

"Yeah?" Evan's eyes narrowed suspiciously. "They seemed to spend a lot of time talking to you."

"Well, you can read all about it in the Hatter's Cove Gazette's next edition," Hayden said.

Suddenly, a young female's voice cried out, "He's dead? You've got to be kidding me!" I turned to see Tiffany Wallace talking to a couple of cops. She looked both disgusted and bewildered at the same time as she crossed her arms and leaned against the squad car.

I moved to the side as Evan and a few other reporters I recognized from the news stations, practically trampled me on their way to the irritated young woman.

CHAPTER FIVE

I SLAMMED ANOTHER drawer shut. Four days had passed since Benny Yates died, and I was starting to get a little antsy waiting around for information. Luke had been less helpful than normal. He had always been tight lipped about any cases he was working on, but usually he would have had something he could share with me officially by now. The only thing I had been able to get out of him was that the wheels of justice in Hatter's Cove moved much slower than it did in Miami, and I would just have to be patient.

I blew out my breath, pushing my bangs out and away from my eyes, as I continued to dig through old newspapers. *Just how did a healthy twenty-four year old man with no known drug history, as I finally learned, drop dead in the back of an alley behind his place of employment?* A quick look at the body, while I was waiting for police, told me that, he hadn't been stabbed or shot, so it had to be something else. And that something else, my gut was telling me, wasn't natural. Slamming the drawer I was working in shut, I dropped to my haunches, and opened the bottom drawer.

A pair of brown loafers appeared in the corner of my vision. "Have I mentioned how much I hate your organizational system, Hayden?"

"Not in the last hour," he said from the doorway to the file room, where every paper since the founding of the Gazette over a hundred years ago could be found.

I spared a second to glance up at him. "When I interned here during high school, I had these drawers organized. They were a thing of beauty. Each paper was in order by date, and I had created a detailed finding aid, which laid out the important town events and dates on which they occurred." I waved my hand over the drawer. "What happened?"

"Our last publisher and editor thought they should be organized by major events in the town's history. For instance, hurricane's are over here," he said slapping his hand against the metal cabinet nearest him, before pointing at the filing cabinet in front of me. "You're currently looking through alligator and shark attacks."

I sat back on my heels. *Well, that explained the unusual amount of shark attack headlines I was seeing throughout the filing cabinet.* "What about non-animal related deaths?"

"We have a section that covers the deaths of local people that were important to the town over there," he said gesturing to the cabinet at the end of the row.

Figuring James Wallace counted as an important death, I moved over to the end cabinet. "Why haven't these things been digitized, yet?"

"Are you volunteering?" he said in amusement.

Not even dignifying that question with an answer, I dropped to my knees and opened a drawer that covered the last ten years.

"What are you looking for anyway?"

"Information about James Wallace's death."

"Oh, that would be over in the major town trials section." He tapped on the filing cabinet standing next to the hurricane cabinet. "Everything related to James Wallace's death would be in here."

I looked up at him in disbelief. "What happens when two different important events occurs on the same day?"

"We'll cross that bridge when we come to it," he said with a chuckle. "As soon as I can afford an intern, I'll have everything put back in order." Crossing his arms, he leaned against the hurricane cabinet. "Why are you so interested in James Wallace's death?"

"I heard that he was murdered by his daughter, Tiffany Wallace."

"He was. It was a shame. I liked him."

"You knew him?"

"I covered a few events at the country club when he was Chairman there. He was always nice to me. I didn't know him well, but I do know that he absolutely adored his daughter. After her mother died in childbirth, she was all that he had. It was rather shocking when they arrested her for murder." He fell silent as I continued to search.

"Finally!" I pulled out one of the papers and laid it flat on the table behind me. I gently lifted up the paper to reveal a few holes and gnawed edges. I raised my eyebrow. "The rats?" At Hayden's nod, I asked, "How's Rooster?"

"Good. He's back at the vet now. He had a slight infection in his missing eye, but she thinks he's going to be okay. She also thinks he's been living on the street for quite a while, probably since he was a kitten."

"He's too friendly to be wild," I pointed out.

"He didn't have a collar or a microchip, so he's ours until someone else claims him. The vet said I should be able to pick him up this afternoon."

Smiling, I laid the paper out on the desk. "Let's see. Tiffany poisoned her father on her eighteenth birthday."

"She supposedly put strychnine in his scotch. To everyone's shock, she pled guilty to manslaughter after two days of testimony, right before the case was supposed to go to the jury. She cried the whole time she was before the judge. I don't think she actually wanted to plead guilty, but her lawyer talked her into it."

"Simon said that Evan believed she paid the prosecutor and judge off to get the charge reduced."

"The prosecutor, Frank Taylor, was disbarred a few years after the trial for doing as much on another case." He shook his head. "But I don't think Taylor took a bribe to reduce the charges on this particular case."

"Why?"

"Well, in my opinion, the evidence against Tiffany wasn't very strong. No one could put her at the scene of the crime and she had an alibi." He made a face. "Well, sort of. The alibi was rather shaky but I think Taylor reduced the charge to manslaughter, because he was worried the jury would find her not guilty. He paid for it in the election that year. The people voted him out in a landslide. Evan's articles on the murder stirred up the whole community against Tiffany, and they wanted her head on a silver platter, so when he didn't deliver, they turned on him. Anyway, when her lawyer finally convinced her to plead guilty, Taylor jumped at it. He couldn't wait to get her before the judge."

"Do you think she was guilty?"

"I don't know. I do know that she shouldn't have pled guilty. I spoke to the jury members after it was over . . . at least two of them had a hard time believing she killed her father. They said that for them, there was just too much reasonable doubt. Personally, I think they just didn't like her father. The way James Wallace was portrayed by the defense *and* the prosecution wasn't very flattering. He came across as a very cold and unfeeling man. The strange thing was that the only person who objected to that portrayal was Tiffany. I overheard her tell her lawyer during the trial that she'd fire him and represent herself, if he continued to let people think her father was a bad man."

I glanced at the big black and white picture of Tiffany arriving at the courthouse the morning of the trial. She was clutching at Benny's shirt and looking up at him fearfully, as he led her up the courthouse steps.

"Have you been able to find out how Benny died?" Hayden asked. "Rumor has it that Chief Waltrip suspects it was a drug overdose, possibly heroin."

Smiling, I waved my hand dismissively. "I don't know where he got that idea. To tell you the truth, I think Chief Waltrip's a bit out of his depth. With any luck, they'll put Luke Casey on it." I hated to admit it, but Luke Casey was a good cop. An excellent cop, and if anyone could figure out what was going on, it was him.

Hayden looked down at the coffee cup in his hand. "I heard that Detective Casey was from Miami."

"Yep," I said, still reading Evan Quincy's article on the trial.

"You two know each other?"

"Hmm?" I glanced back at him. "Oh, yeah, we go way back." I looked back down at the paper. "It says here that someone overheard Tiffany plot to kill her father, but it doesn't say who."

"One of Evan's confidential sources."

"Did he tell you who his source was?"

Hayden shook his head. "Evan and I have never been close."

"Did they really think she murdered her father because he wouldn't let her marry Benny Yates?"

Hayden shrugged. "Love is blind. Especially young love and she was in love with Benny Yates. Very much so. If you add in the fact that her father tried to put a stop to their love, the cops theorized that it just made her want him even more. Besides, people have killed to protect their inheritance before. Wallace threatened to disinherit her if she didn't stop seeing Benny. He died a few hours later."

"Did James Wallace make good on his threat before he died?"

"No, but it doesn't matter. Florida has a slayer statute, which says that murderers can't profit from their killings. Everything went to the next beneficiary."

"Let me guess. Vivian Wallace."

"That's right."

"I wonder how she and Tiffany are getting along, now that Tiffany's been released?"

"I suspect good."

"Really?" I asked in surprise. "That's surprising. If it was my husband who was murdered, I'd be pretty angry at whoever killed him."

"Vivian supported Tiffany throughout the trial. She never believed Tiffany was guilty." He glanced over my shoulder at the paper and shook his head. "James Wallace's death is ancient history."

"Maybe."

He moved the paper to the side with one index finger. "You do have other things to do, you know."

Wondering if he had anything else to do, I moved the paper back in front of me. "I'm taking a break."

"Just how long is this break? I have yet to see your latest column on the Sea Urchin's new sandwich on my desk, and I've been waiting for it for the last two days. Now, I don't want your usual type of column. Try to be tactful."

I gave him a baleful stare. "You want me to lie."

"No, I don't want you to lie, I just want you to be . . . diplomatic in your phrasing."

* * *

I hit my backspace button again, wiping out my last line. Asparagus. How I despise it with every fiber of my being. I felt a hand grab the back of my chair. I resisted the urge to look back into Hayden's green eyes. He was hanging around, peering over my shoulder so often that I was starting to enjoy his presence a bit too much. "There is nothing good about asparagus, and what sadist would think of putting it into a sandwich?" I complained, as I put the finishing touches on my review of the Crispy Sea Urchin's latest offering to the Hatter's Cove community.

"Oh, I don't know, it's not that bad. I kind of like asparagus."

I whipped my head around and looked back at Detective Casey. "You would." I turned around in my chair. A personal visit from the police department. That meant either I was being arrested, or they had information to share. Considering that I had been behaving myself lately, I could only assume that Luke was here about Benny Yate's death. As far as I was concerned, it was about time.

His eyes narrowed as he read what was on my computer screen. "That's a bit harsh, isn't it?"

"Oh, what did she write now?" Hayden asked from his office doorway. He looked over at me in exasperation. "Do you remember that conversation we had about tact, at all?"

Ignoring Hayden, I minimized my screen and reached for my notebook. "Well, what's going on, Detective? Do you know what killed Benny Yates, yet?"

Luke leaned back against Simon's desk and looked at me for a long uncomfortable moment. He spared a glance at Hayden, before carefully reaching into the inside of his suit coat, and bringing out a plastic baggy containing one of Dolly's pink and green cookie bags. He held the baggy out in front of me. "Do you recognize this, Kat?"

"It's one of Dolly's bags. I'm assuming it's the one Benny was holding when he died."

"We found a heart shaped sticker with your name written on it," Luke said softly.

I snapped my notebook shut. *Huh, maybe he was here to arrest me.* "Can I see it?"

He leaned forward and held the bag under my nose.

Hayden spoke first. "I recognize that," he said as he pulled up a chair and sat down next to me. "That's the bag you brought back from the Cookie Jar grand opening."

"Are you sure?" Luke asked in surprise.

I nodded in agreement. "Positive." I pointed to the slight tare in the corner of the bag. "I tore the corner when I opened it up that afternoon."

Luke frowned as he folded the bag up and placed it back into his pocket. "You're absolutely sure?"

"Absolutely. Dolly gave it to me just before I left the Cookie Jar. She said it was a new recipe and wanted me to be the first to try it."

"She did? Well, that was nice of her," Luke said. "Hmm. Well, that changes things a bit. I assumed Benny was about to deliver the bag to you." His dark blue eyes narrowed suspiciously. "If you had the bag, then how did it get into Benny's hands?"

I glanced behind Luke, toward Simon's desk. *Just how did the bag get to Benny?* Feeling Hayden shift closer to me, I brought my attention back to the detective. "I don't know. That's strange. I didn't give it to him."

Luke tilted his head before glancing over his shoulder. "Is there something you want to tell me?"

"No." I glanced back at Simon's desk. *Just what did Simon do with that bag?*

"Really?" Luke asked. "Then why do you keep looking behind me?"

My eyes flew back to Luke's. "You are so suspicious."

Hayden shook his head. "She gave the bag to Simon Sayors. He works here at the Gazette."

I snapped my fingers. "Oh, that's right. I did."

"Simon Sayors," Luke said. "That's the fellow that fought with Benny Yates just before he died."

"Not *just* before," I pointed out quickly. "It was several hours before actually. He had nothing to do with Benny's death."

Luke raised his eyebrow. "And just where is Simon right now?"

Hayden shifted uneasily in his chair. "He called in sick today." I noticed Hayden failed to mention that Simon had called in sick every day since Benny's death.

"How long has he been sick?" Luke asked sharply.

"A couple of days." Hayden said. "Why, is that important?"

Luke didn't answer. "Did he eat any of the cookies?"

"More than likely," I said. "What's wrong?"

Luke reached into his pocket, pulled out his cell phone, and walked out of the room.

Hayden looked down at me. "What's going on?"

I shrugged helplessly as Luke came back in. He pointed at me with his cell phone. "Did you eat any of the cookies?"

"No."

His eyes narrowed. "Why not?"

"I had spent over three hours eating every kind of cookie, cake, and candy, imaginable that day. If I had any more, I probably would have died from sugar overload. Besides, I was sure I gained ten pounds by just walking through the Cookie Jar's door."

Luke's eyes widened slightly. "Good."

"What did Benny die of?" Hayden asked.

Luke hesitated. "He was poisoned."

Hayden crossed his arms. "Poisoned? By what?"

"The chocolate crème filled cookies in the bag contained strychnine," Luke answered.

Strychnine. The same poison that killed James Wallace. I glanced back at Hayden. "Good thing you didn't eat one."

Hayden reached for my phone.

"Who are you calling?" Luke asked.

"I'm checking on Simon," Hayden said. A few seconds later, he left a terse message on Simon's answering machine to call him back.

"Don't worry," Luke said, as Hayden hung up, "I've already sent someone to check on him. Did you talk to him today?"

"Yes, he called me a few hours ago," Hayden said.

"He's probably all right then," Luke said gently. "There was enough strychnine in those cookies to kill three or four people. If he had eaten one, he'd be dead by now. We'll check him out just to be safe though."

Suddenly concerned, I leaned forward. "What's going on, Luke? Usually, I don't get this much information from you until the press conference, which," I said leaning over and checking my calendar, "oh yeah, hasn't been scheduled yet."

"We're working on it," Luke said with a grimace. "We have reason to suspect that Benny Yates' death was accidental."

"He was *accidentally* poisoned to death, with strychnine?" Hayden asked. "Just how did that happen?"

"When he ate the cookies meant for someone else." Luke looked down at me. "Your name was on the bag. I'm afraid to ask, but do you have any enemies, Kat?"

CHAPTER SIX

"DREAMS DO NOT die, but you should," Hayden read aloud. "Another restaurant owner?" He dropped the letter down on the conference room table where we had spread out all of my recent *fan* mail, as I liked to call it.

I shook my head. "Disgruntled singer. That one came from one of the advice columns. He wrote in asking if he should follow his dream to become a pop singer, or work at his parent's bait shop like his family wants. I told him to give up and move on."

He picked up another letter written on pink stationary. "How could you know he was a bad singer from the letter?"

"If he was good, he wouldn't be writing in asking if he should give up or not. Besides, I know him. He's my cousin, Jimmy. Trust me, he's not good. He sounds a bit like a high-pitched seal in pain. They threw food at him at the last place he tried to play at a week ago. He got a concussion from all the rolls that they aimed at his head."

He cocked his head to the side. "The rolls were hard enough to give him a concussion?" he asked in disbelief.

"You never really read my columns, do you?" I asked in exasperation. "Jimmy did a gig at the Biker Baker's Half-Dozen Bar and Sea-food Grill. They were the subject of one of my first reviews. I spent three paragraphs on their rolls alone. I wrote that the only thing more punishing than listening to the sub-par wailings coming from their so-called musical acts, was trying to bite into their rolls. I then said they should change the name on the menu from Bubba's Buttery Blues Soft Rolls, to Bubba's Buttery Rock n Rolls. At least then it wouldn't be false advertising."

Hayden shook his head. "I just can't imagine why anyone would want to poison you."

"Hey, I chipped a molar on those things. Besides, I don't think any of these people," I said waving my hand across the mounds of mail on the table, "poisoned those cookies."

"You heard Casey. He believes that the poisoned cookies in the bag were meant for you."

"I sincerely doubt anyone was trying to kill me."

"Weren't you the one worried about someone poisoning you just last week?"

I laughed. "Well, yeah. I was afraid someone was going to put something nasty in the dishes they served me, but I never thought it was going to be strychnine." I snapped my fingers. "I know. Maybe all the restaurateurs and bakers got together and decided to do me in." I lifted up my cousin's letter. "Jimmy's probably the ring leader."

"I'm glad you're taking this so seriously." He looked toward the open door. "Simon?"

I turned as Simon walked in with a hangdog look on his face.

"Where have you been?" Hayden asked. "The police dropped by your apartment this morning and you weren't there."

Simon shuffled his feet. "I know. They picked me up an hour ago."

"Where were you?" I asked.

Simon glanced up. "Well, I started to feel better, so I went out."

"Out where?" Hayden asked.

Simon looked down and mumbled something.

"Where?"

"I said the movies," he admitted a bit louder.

"You were playing hooky?" I asked with a laugh.

"I really was sick," Simon protested.

"What were your symptoms?" Hayden crossed his arms and glared at me as though I was somehow responsible. I crossed my arms and glared back as Simon rattled off his symptoms.

"Horrible sore throat. Worst I've ever had. You heard me on the phone, Hayden. I could barely talk. And my nose still hurt from where Benny had hit me. You said that I should just stay home and rest. Remember?"

"You sound okay now," Hayden pointed out.

"Well, I took a nap." Simon rubbed his throat. "I also drank some hot tea with honey. That helped a lot."

"Honey is a super food," I helpfully pointed out.

"Doesn't sound much like strychnine poisoning," Hayden said with a relieved sigh.

Simon's features twisted. "It's not. I tried to tell them it was nothing but a little cold, but they still insisted I go to the doctor." He looked up nervously. "While I was at the hospital, they got a search warrant for my apartment."

I sat up straighter. "Did they give you a copy?"

Simon reached into his messenger bag. I eagerly grabbed the warrant out of his hand and laid it out on the desk.

"Why do you want it?" Simon asked.

I read the warrant, as Hayden explained that the warrant would have to lay out what the police were searching for.

I tapped my finger on the piece of paper. "Well, they were looking for everything and the proverbial kitchen sink, but specifically they were looking for poison and syringes."

"They think I killed Benny." Simon turned frightened eyes to Hayden. "I didn't. I swear."

Hayden stood up and patted the young man on his back. "Don't worry, they're just running down any leads they have right now."

"Did you go straight home after you left here on Friday?" I asked.

Simon shook his head. "I felt bad about what happened at Miss Dolly's, so I asked Beatrix to drop me off at the Cookie Jar to apologize. I figured I would just walk home from there, since I only live a few blocks away. Only the Cookie Jar was closed for repairs. I was just about to leave when Rich Fairchild came out. He said not to worry. No one blamed me and that Miss Dolly was going to fire Benny."

"What happened to the cookies that I gave you?" I asked.

"I don't know," Simon said. "I remember I had it when I walked to the Cookie Jar looking for Miss Dolly. I got tired and sat down for a few seconds at one of the outside tables. My nose was still killing me. I guess I left them on the table."

"Did you eat any of them?"

"Just one," Simon said. "It was delicious."

I looked over at Hayden. "See?"

"See what?"

"No one was after me. If the cookies had been poisoned, he would be dead right now."

"But they were poisoned," Hayden said, "The police tested them."

I shrugged. "They had to have been poisoned after Simon lost them."

"They think someone was trying to kill you?" Simon asked. "But why would anyone want to hurt you?"

Hayden held up a handful of letters. "These are just from this month."

I pushed his hand down. "Tell me something, Simon. Did Benny think Tiffany murdered her father?"

Hayden sat down next to me. "Tiffany Wallace again?"

"She's accused of poisoning her father with strychnine, and then it turns out the cookies that killed her boyfriend are laced with strychnine too. That's just a tad too coincidental to me."

Simon shook his head vehemently. "It can't be Tiffany this time. I was with her all evening, until she left to pick up Benny at eleven-fifty the night he died."

Hayden and I looked at him in surprise. "You were with her all evening?" I asked.

"Yeah, she had stopped by the Cookie Jar while I was there, looking for Benny. I forgot how sweet she could be. As soon as she saw me, she ran up and apologized for Benny's behavior. We ended up having lunch together, and then made plans to meet up after she ran some errands. She was with me from five o'clock until just before midnight."

I raised my eyebrow. Fast mover, our Simon. "Are you and she a couple now?"

Simon blushed. "Oh no, nothing like that. I think she just wanted to talk. She doesn't have any other friends. I got the feeling she's very lonely. Benny called her while we were talking, and told her that he was going to have to lie low because the police were after him, and to pick him up at midnight. She asked if she could hang out with me until then. We ended up just watching TV until she left."

"Did you think about calling the police and letting them know that he was going to be at the Cookie Jar at midnight?" Hayden asked.

"No," Simon said, "I didn't want to upset Tiffany. She and Benny obviously had plans for that night, and she was pretty upset about it as it was."

"I thought she and Benny had broken up after she was sent away," Hayden said.

"They had," Simon said. "He was convinced she was guilty and didn't want anything else to do with her."

I passed the warrant back to Simon. "Then why had they made plans to spend Valentine's Day together?"

"She said he finally believed her."

"Really?" I asked. "What made him change his opinion?"

"I don't know. To tell you the truth, I'm starting to think she may have been innocent, too. You should have seen her when she started to talk about her dad. She was really upset."

Hayden looked over at me. "Benny told you he was about to right a wrong. Perhaps, the wrong had something to do with Tiffany being accused of her dad's murder."

I nodded. "I think that's a strong possibility."

Hayden tapped his fingers against the table. "So do I." He patted the left side of his chest as a sudden vibration came from the inside of his suit coat.

I turned away and faced Simon as Hayden answered the phone. "Can you get me an interview with Tiffany?"

"An interview? Sure. Why?"

My heart sank a little. "Because she might be innocent." When he gave me another blank look, I added sadly, "It would probably make for a good story."

"Oh," he said enthusiastically, "that would be great. I always liked her."

"Do you know where she's living right now?"

"With her step-mother. Vivian took her back in as soon as she was released."

"Simon," Hayden said turning off his phone and dropping it into his pocket, "go talk to Tiffany."

I quickly wrapped my arm around Simon's thin shoulders. "Simon just asked me if I could tag along."

"You do realize that I'm standing right here, don't you?" Hayden asked in exasperation. "I didn't hear him say any such thing."

"We were just talking about it while you were on the phone. Simon thought it would be a good idea to talk to her and asked me if I could tag along. He felt she might be more willing to talk to another female."

"I did?" Simon asked.

I let my fingers dig into his shoulder, hoping he would get the hint.

Simon winced. "Why are you pinching me?"

I patted Simon's arm. *Not too terribly quick on the uptake, our Simon, but sweet, nevertheless.*

Hayden shook his head. "Somehow, I have a feeling she'll be just as willing to talk to him. I have somewhere else I want you to go."

"Where to now?" I leaned my head back as I tried to remember where I had put my Tums.

"Chief Waltrip just called a news conference. They've made an arrest in Benny Yates' murder. I figured you'd want to be there."

* * *

Chief Waltrip stood at the podium and gripped its sides tightly. "We have charged Dolly Fairchild with the murder of Benedict Yates."

I let out a surprised gasp. I glanced over at Luke standing off to the side. He looked about as sick as I felt. I noticed a subtle shake of his head as he looked at me. I wondered if it was a warning to keep quiet, or a hint that he disagreed with his chief. When he turned his baby blues toward Waltrip with a disgusted look on his handsome face, I figured it was the latter.

Evan Quincy raised his hand. "Not Tiffany Wallace?"

"Miss Wallace is not a suspect in this crime," the chief bellowed out.

Evan's eyebrows rose all the way up to his widow's peak in surprise. He cleared his throat. "But the strychnine—"

"Miss Wallace isn't the only person in the history of the world who has used strychnine to kill someone. It is our belief that Mrs. Fairchild used that method to point suspicion toward Miss Wallace."

A reporter from the five o'clock news raised her hand. "Do you have a motive yet, Chief?"

"We have reason to believe that Mr. Yates was not the intended target."

I raised my hand. "And who was the intended target?"

Chief Waltrip's eyes narrowed. "I believe you have been informed of that already, Ms. Archer. Next question."

I felt my fellow reporter's eyes focus in on me.

I kept my hand up in the air. "And just why would Dolly Fairchild want to kill me?"

Waltrip scowled. "You have quite the reputation, Ms. Archer."

I ignored the snickers of the reporters around me.

"We believe Mrs. Fairchild was worried about the column you were about to write on her grand opening. Fearing a negative review, she decided to poison the cookies meant for you."

It was my turn to snicker. "Are you saying that she was so afraid of negative publicity that she purposely poisoned her *own* cookies?"

"As I am sure the crime reporters here know, criminals don't always think things through. We, by and large, do not deal with criminal geniuses. Mrs. Fairchild obviously felt she could get away with it."

"Did she confess?" Evan asked.

"No, she did not, but we have more than enough evidence to show that she willfully and with malicious aforethought, poisoned her cookies and personally delivered them to her intended target with the hopes of causing her death."

Being her intended target, I raised my hand once again. "One of my co-workers ate one of the cookies and lived to tell the tale. How do you explain that?"

Waltrip glared at me. "Obviously, not every cookie was poisoned. Your co-worker was very lucky. So, were you. Written inside the bag was a little message just for you, Ms. Archer. You were a very lucky young lady. Very lucky."

CHAPTER SEVEN

"A LITTLE PRESENT just for you, Kitty Kat,' is not a threat, Luke." I sat down at the picnic table and turned to watch the waves crash down on the beach.

Luke sat down across from me. He dropped his lunch down on the table before shrugging out of his suit jacket, revealing a nice wide chest, thick biceps, and a brown leather shoulder holster complete with one very large gun. I watched as three girls passed by, their eyes riveted on Luke as they walked and wondered if it was the man or the gun that had their undivided attention. When one tripped over a piece of driftwood lying on the beach, I figured it was probably the man.

I turned my attention back to Luke, as he picked up a ketchup bottle and squirted a line down his hot dog, completely oblivious to his affect on the women walking around him. "I know that," he said. "You know that, but Chief Waltrip, however, is convinced it's a threat."

"That's ridiculous. Dolly wouldn't hurt me. She's one of my mother's best friends. If she were going to kill me, it would have been when I accidentally broke two of her china plates when I was nine. She barely batted an eye. I was afraid my mother was about to murder me, but that's another story. Dolly didn't try to poison me or anyone else."

Luke held up his hands. "I don't think she did either, but police work is different here in Hatter's Cove. As soon as Chief Waltrip saw all those death threats you had received, and heard that Dolly had made those cookies for you personally, well, he was off and running." He picked up his hot dog and took a large bite.

"How can you eat that? It looks green." I felt my features contort in disgust. Pink or red I could see, but this thing was a grayish green.

He held the hot dog out to me. "Try it, you might like it."

"No thanks." I pushed his hand away and took a drink of my coke. "You people have a huge chain of evidence problem. You know that, don't you?"

"Yes, I do. Dolly's attorney spent a few precious billable minutes telling me the exact same thing. I'm going to tell you what I told him."

"Which is?"

He washed his next bite down with a huge gulp of soda. "Talk to Chief Waltrip or the prosecutor. I have nothing to do with this."

I dropped my sunglasses down on the table and pinched the bridge of my nose. "But you're in charge of the investigation."

"Correction. The chief is in charge. I'm just the new guy. This isn't Miami. We do things differently here in Hatter's Cove," he said doing a fair imitation of the Chief's voice.

"Speaking of Miami."

He groaned and rolled his eyes. "I wondered how long it would take for you to start prying. You are so nosy."

"That's why I became a reporter. I figured I should get paid for my natural inclinations." I looked at him in concern. The night before in the alley, I had thought he looked a little weaker than what I remembered, but now in the bright daylight, it was obvious something was wrong. "Are you all right, Luke?"

"I'm getting there. I'm surprised you didn't call someone in Miami and ask why I had left."

"I figured I'd get it out of you sooner or later. What happened?"

"I got shot two months ago," he said matter-of-factly. "I was undercover and . . . things went bad." He glanced over at the ocean. "I decided to go somewhere else, somewhere a little less dangerous than Miami. I saw that the Hatter's Cove Police Department was looking for a detective and I applied. It's just my luck I was greeted with a dead body on my first day at the job. And of course, there was you. I don't know what was more frightening," he teased.

Realizing that teasing me was his way of trying to deflect my attention away from whatever happened in Miami; I smiled accordingly, and promptly changed the subject back to Benny Yate's death. "You still don't have any idea how the cookies got from Simon to Benny. Anyone could have tampered with them after Simon lost the bag."

His eyes narrowed. "If he lost it. How well do you know Simon?"

"Well enough to know he'd never try to kill anyone. Please tell me you have some other suspect besides Dolly or Simon."

"It would help if we knew who the intended victim was."

"I think you can rule me out as a victim, potential or otherwise."

He looked at me intently. "Good. Let's keep it that way." He pointed his finger at me. "If you even get the hint that something's wrong, you call me."

"Yes, sir, officer sir, on one condition."

He dropped his head to the table and groaned. "What?"

"What do you know about Benny Yates?"

Luke lifted his head and swiped a napkin across his lips. "Not much. Benny mostly kept out of trouble. He worked twenty hours a week at the courthouse, and picked up a little extra cash working for Dolly Fairchild or Vivian Wallace on the side."

"Vivian? What does he do for her?"

"That's what I would like to figure out. According to Vivian, he just ran little errands for her. Helped out around the house. Have you seen her house?" He didn't wait for an answer before adding, "She has a maid that comes four times a week, gardeners who show up twice a week, and a chauffer to take her anywhere she wants to go . . . so what did she need him for?"

"I don't know."

Luke gave me a crooked grin. "Yeah, but you're going to find out soon."

"Have you suddenly turned psychic, Detective?"

"I don't have to be psychic to know that you'll ferret out that little nugget soon enough."

Ferret? I've been called worse. "All right. As soon as I find out, I'll give you a call. But I expect the same courtesy. I want the chain of information to flow freely my way, as well. I have another question I want you to answer."

"Just be careful. The last time you investigated a story I was working on, I had to arrest you for obstruction."

"Bah, trumped up charges."

"You stole evidence."

"I did not steal. I was protecting the evidence." I felt the need to repeat the most important word in my sentence. "Protecting. If it wasn't for me, it would have been destroyed."

"Fine. What do you want to ask?" he asked with a wary look in his eyes.

"I should have gotten a medal."

"Whatever. What is your question?"

"At least a key to the city."

"You're not going to get anything if you don't tell me what it is you want to know."

"Do you know how many of the cookies Benny had eaten?"

"He had a half eaten one in his hand and the coroner thought he had eaten another. Why?"

"Just curious. I remember seeing four in the bag. Simon had one and Benny had two. So, who ate the other one?"

"That's a good question." He pointed a warning finger at me. "And if you figure it out before I do . . .?"

"You'll be the first I call." *Right after Hayden gives me the go ahead to publish the information in the Gazette.* I looked over at Luke staring pensively out at the ocean. "Okay, what are you holding back? I know you, there's something else you're not telling me."

Luke nervously bobbed his leg up and down as he turned to look at me. "Okay, look I don't usually . . . the only reason I'm telling you these things is because there still is the chance you may be a target, and since you know these people, you might be able to help me." He looked at me, severe pain radiating across his face as he said, "You're the only one I can trust."

I pressed my hand to my heart and grinned. "Oh my."

He closed his eyes. "Don't make me regret saying that."

"You trust me. I think I'm going to cry, Detective."

"I knew I was going to regret saying anything."

I leaned forward. "What do you have?"

"Okay, but this is off the record until I give you the okay to print. Understand?" Once I gave my agreement, he added, "Benny had over fifty thousand dollars in his savings account."

"Where did he get that much money?"

"As near as we can tell, he didn't inherit it, and he didn't work for it, so your guess is as good as mine. All we know is he made monthly lump sum deposits."

"Since when?"

"He opened the account last April with fifteen thousand dollars in cash, but he could have been sitting on that money for awhile. We just don't know."

"Hmm. Do you have anything else?"

Luke shook his head.

"That's it?" I asked in disappointment.

"What do you want from me? Things move slowly in Hatter's Cove." Luke swiveled around, lifted up his long legs, and threw them over the bench. He walked over to the trashcan and threw away what was left of his lunch, before sauntering over to the table. He picked up his suit jacket and wrapped it over his arm. "Be careful, Kat."

"You too," I said as I waved bye.

* * *

"Hey, Kat, I want you to get over to the car wash on Fountain Boulevard. Someone's been stealing the quarters out of the machine," Hayden called out from his office. "Interview the owner."

I paused typing long enough to glare at him over my shoulder. "What about Beatrix? Can't she handle it?" I looked over at her desk. Her *empty* desk. "Where is she, by the way?"

Hayden pursed his lips for a few seconds. "She's taking some time off."

"Again?"

"Yep," he said with some bite.

I turned around in my chair. *Could it be? Is the Queen about to be deposed?* "Isn't this her second vacation this month? It's seems rather excessive."

"Why are you complaining?" Hayden asked dryly. He leaned his shoulder against the doorframe. "Haven't you enjoyed the peace and quiet?"

"She's mad that she didn't get assigned the Benny Yate's story, isn't she?" Beatrix had made her displeasure known in many subtle passive-aggressive ways, since Hayden informed her in no uncertain terms that I would be covering the story. It didn't take a genius to figure out that her temper was going to boil over sooner or later.

Hayden's features clouded. "She'll get over it."

"Where is she now?"

"I don't know. Why do you care?"

"She's a co-worker. I'm interested in her life."

"Well, she's not news, so get uninterested. You've been begging for a big story for a while now, and I'm just about to give you one."

I restrained myself from laughing in his face. I did not consider a nickel and dime theft from the car wash a big story. Besides, I had a story. More importantly, I had a murder. Two in fact. Benny Yates and James Wallace. The only question on my mind was who killed Benny, and whether his murder had anything to do with James Wallace's death. That was my story, and I was just about to tell Hayden as much when Simon walked in, happy as the proverbial clam.

He raised his hands above his head as though he had just scored the winning touchdown. "I solved it. I know what happened to Benny."

Hayden and I descended on him at once. "What did Tiffany have to say?"

Simon dropped his messenger bag on the desk and held out his hands. "A lot. I have a great angle on Benny's death. Get this." Simon spread his arms wide. "Suicide."

"Suicide?" Hayden asked. "But the coroner has ruled it a murder."

"That's already been done. Everyone else is already covering the murder angle. Absolutely no one else is thinking suicide." Simon's face lit up like a Christmas tree. "It's different, right?"

Different was definitely the word. Glancing between Simon to Hayden, I bit my lip, and then cleared my throat delicately.

Hayden ignored me. "Simon, there's a reason why no one else is thinking suicide."

I coughed delicately and tried to get my editor's attention.

He steadfastly refused to look at me. Smiling gently, Hayden said patiently, "Benny was murdered. That's a fact."

I coughed a bit more loudly, pleased that I finally had his attention.

"Do you need a cough drop?" he asked wryly before turning back to Simon. "Why do you think Benny committed suicide?"

"Because Tiffany said he was really upset that day. First, there was the fight with Evan. Then he fought with me. Then he was fired by Dolly. Then the police were out looking for him," Simon said, "and *then*, he got into a fight with Rich Fairchild. Tiffany said that Benny busted his nose, too."

"Why?" Hayden and I asked simultaneously.

Simon blinked. "Oh, I didn't ask. Why? Do you think that was important?"

I watched in amusement as Hayden's eyes widened. "Perhaps, just a bit," he said softly. My purse was already in my hand when Hayden spared a second to glance at me. He turned back to Simon. "Okay, Simon, I want you to go to Fountain Boulevard, you," he said, pointing a finger at me, "go speak to Tiffany."

CHAPTER EIGHT

"BENNY HATED COFFEE. Absolutely despised the stuff. I baked him a mocha flavored chocolate cake for his sixteenth birthday and he spit it out. He said that coffee and chocolate together was an abomination." Tiffany Wallace's face clouded, as she laid out a plate of brownies on Vivian Wallace's glass topped kitchen table.

"Benny certainly had strong views, didn't he?" I laid my notebook flat on the table and underlined Benny Yate's name.

"I just don't understand why he ate those cookies." She pushed the plate toward me and looked at me expectantly. When I hesitated, she added, "Everyone has been bringing me food since Benny died. I have to get rid of this stuff somehow."

Resigned, I reached forward and picked up a brownie, surprised to find that it was absolutely delicious. "Who brought these?"

"Dolly did right before that fool sheriff arrested her. I have some red velvet petit fours from Vivian you should try." She stood up, opened a cabinet, and brought out a blue round box tied up with a pink ribbon. She opened the top and shoved the box my way. "I also have some fruit, if you would prefer that," she said wryly, as she waved her hand toward the five baskets of fruit sitting on top of the white marble countertops. "Or perhaps, you would like a casserole. I have plenty of that, too. Vivian took some of it to the shelter this morning, but it still keeps coming." She popped a brownie into her mouth. "I don't understand why people keep bringing me all this food. It's not like I relied on Benny to feed me." Her blue-grey eyes narrowed suspiciously, as she tucked her light brown hair behind her ear. "I'm even getting food from people that I know hate me."

I glanced at my brownie worriedly. "Dolly wouldn't be on that list."

Tiffany shook her head. "No. Dolly's very sweet. She was one of the few that believed I was innocent. I don't believe for a second that she killed Benny. Frankly, that's the only reason I'm talking to you right now. If there's any way I can help, please let me know." She glanced back at the mountain of food piled up around the kitchen. "I just wish they would stop bringing me food."

I happily shoved the last bite into my mouth before saying, "It's customary when a loved one dies to bring food to those in grief."

Tiffany made a face. "I think people are just trying to get on Vivian's good side. She made a big deal at the country club about how everyone should accept me back into society. Money is always a great motivator, and Vivian has more than enough to get what she wants. Besides, Benny wasn't exactly a loved one."

"Really?" I scribbled through the heart I drew on the pad of paper.

"Oh, don't get me wrong. I cared for Benny a great deal. I was even madly in love with him at one time, but that was a long time ago. Things changed," she added softly before adding, "I'm upset that he's dead. Very upset. You don't know how upset I am. I'm probably more upset than anyone by this. No one could be more upset than I am.

This whole thing is very, very . . ." she hesitated as she fought to come up with an appropriate word.

"Upsetting?" I asked writing down the word and drawing a circle around it three times.

She nodded. "Very upsetting. I'm just not happy about this, at all."

Thinking that Benny probably wasn't too happy with how things turned out either, I said, "You seem to be holding up pretty well for someone who lost her ex-boyfriend to a dessert."

"Thank you. Benny may have been a rude, inconsiderate, selfish, coldhearted dweeb, with the manners of a pig and the looks of a troll doll—"

"Can I quote you?" I asked as I jotted down her description.

"Absolutely," she said. "But despite all of that, he had one thing going for him."

"Which was?"

"He was smart." She leaned forward. "Super smart." She must have been used to people doubting that statement, since she repeated it three more times before adding, "No, really, he was."

"I'll take your word for it," I said, as I wrote 'smart, no really', down on my paper next to his other attributes. "So, you were attracted to his intelligence."

She made a face. "Attracted? Eh, not really. He was helping me with something really important."

"What?"

Tiffany bit her lip. "He was going to help me prove that I wasn't the one who killed my father." Her eyes welled up with tears. "I didn't kill my dad. My attorney convinced me it was best to take the plea." A tear slid down her cheek. "I didn't want to, but he said I'd probably be convicted and would spend the rest of my life in prison if I didn't take the prosecution's offer." She swiped at her cheek and cleared her throat. "Anyway, Benny felt guilty for not believing me, and told me he was going to make it all up to me. He wanted to win back my love. I told him that was impossible. There was too much between us now, but I'd appreciate any help he could give me."

"How was he going to do that?

"He had been snooping around and said he was close to the real killer. I asked him what he meant by that, but he wouldn't tell me. He said he'd explain everything if I went out with him on Valentine's Day. He was nothing, if not persistent. Not to mention a first class jerk. No sooner had I agreed to go out with him, than he called a few hours later and cancelled our date."

"Did Benny say why?"

Tiffany shook her head and then shrugged half-heartedly. "Well, it sort of made sense. The police were still looking for him because he attacked Simon, and destroyed Dolly's display case. Kind of hard to go to a fancy restaurant when you've got warrants out for your arrest. Anyway, when I spoke to him, he told me not to worry; that he was on top of everything, and that I'd be vindicated soon. Then he said to pick him up at midnight at the Cookie Jar." Tiffany smiled. "Simon was with me when Benny called. He's so sweet. He offered to keep me company until it was time to meet Benny. I felt so bad that Benny beat him up. I thought I should smooth things over. I didn't want Benny to go to jail. Not if he was telling me the truth and if he really was close to proving my innocence." She frowned. "Now, he's dead." Her frown turned into a scowl. "And now, I'm never going to be able to prove my innocence or find my father's murderer. Never. I'm just so . . . so very . . ."

I glanced up from my notebook. "Upset?"

She slapped the table with her hand. "Angry!"

"I see that." I doodled an unhappy face next to Tiffany's name. "Do you know who could have killed Benny or why?"

Reaching for her coffee cup, Tiffany shook her head. "I don't know who killed him, but I know why he was killed. He must have figured out who killed my father and framed me. He was silenced to keep him from telling me what he discovered."

"Simon seems to think Benny may have committed suicide."

Tiffany choked on her coffee. As soon as she cleared her throat, she said, "Where in the world did he get that idea? Benny wouldn't kill himself. Trust me; he was too in love with himself and self-absorbed to commit suicide. On his eighteenth birthday, he took me to a tattoo shop to get matching heart shaped tattoos. I got one with his name and I had assumed he was going to get one with my name." She shook her head. "We both walked out with matching I love Benny tattoos. That should have been my first clue."

My eyes widened. "Still, Simon left here under the impression that Benny had been depressed."

Tiffany snorted delicately. "Benny was a naturally unhappy person. Nothing was ever good enough for him. He was doing better. At least he had grown out of his Goth phase." She made a face. "He did seem rather unhappy the day that he died. More so than usual."

"How so?"

"Just . . . nervous. Twitchy. I'm sorry, I wish I had more information to share, but Benny just didn't confide in me. He wanted to do everything himself." She pressed her hand to her heart. "Heaven forbid that I help him in investigating my own father's murder. I was just a girl. You can add sexist down on your list." She waited until I followed her instructions, before adding, "I can't believe I ever loved him and considered marrying him. I guess I was rebelling."

"Did you and your father not get along?"

"See, that's just the thing. We got along perfectly. I still don't understand how anyone could think I could kill my dad. I loved him."

"But you loved Benny, too—at one time," I added quickly as she began to shake her head. "It must have been terribly upsetting when your father objected to your marrying him. What happened the night your father died?"

"We had dinner here at the house. We were celebrating my eighteenth birthday. All of us. Benny, Vivian, Dad, and me. It started out so well, that is, until Benny proposed marriage to me and I accepted. My dad lost it. He just went nuts. I was so embarrassed. I told my dad that I was an adult and that he couldn't tell me what to do. I then told Benny to take me to his apartment. Dad was hollering at us as we drove off. That was the last time I saw him alive." Her eyes welled with tears. "They found his body at the country club a few hours later."

"What did you and Benny do after you left?"

"We went back to his apartment where we spent the next few hours fighting. Benny was furious. He just wouldn't calm down. I got tired of all the drama and went to bed at ten o'clock. I woke up just before midnight to discover the apartment empty. Benny had left a note saying he was going to go have it out with my dad once and for all. I got worried that he was going to do something stupid, so I threw on some clothes and I drove back home as fast as I could."

"I'm surprised Benny wasn't suspected for your father's murder."

"I'm sure he would have been, except by the time he got to the house, Dad had already left for the country club. Vivian said that she sent Benny on his way, but didn't tell him where my father had gone. I showed up a few minutes after he left to go back to the apartment. Vivian spent the next few hours trying to convince me that Benny was an idiot, and that I needed to grow up. We were still arguing when the police came by and said the night watchman at the club found my father's body. They thought I killed my father because he threatened to disinherit me." She shook her head. "Absolutely ridiculous. I wasn't worried. Daddy would have come around. Trust me. I was a daddy's girl through and through. He would have given me whatever I wanted, and at that time, God help me, I wanted Benny. I would never have killed my daddy." She caught my gaze and held, as the tears spilled down her cheeks. "Never."

I looked at her carefully. I had become pretty adept over the years at telling when someone was trying to snow me, and I was about ninety-nine percent certain Tiffany was being sincere. I tapped my pen against the paper considering. *If Tiffany hadn't killed her father—and I was reasonably certain she hadn't—then who did?*

Tiffany dabbed at the corner of her eye with a napkin. "Daddy just wished the best for me. He wanted me to find a nice, sweet, young man who would treat me right. Someone like Simon. I'm sure Daddy would have liked Simon." She looked up at me shyly. "Is Simon seeing anyone right now? He kept mentioning a girl named Rosie. Is he interested in her?"

Surprised at the sudden change in subject, I blinked a few times before artfully stuttering out, "I haven't a clue." Clearing my throat, I pressed on, "Do you have any idea who could have killed your father?"

Tiffany's gaze shifted to the window and the ocean beyond. "Not really, I thought..."

"You thought...," I prompted when she fell silent.

She shook her head and glanced back at me briefly before glancing over her shoulder nervously. "I have no idea. I just really don't know." She ran her hands down her arms as though she was chilled.

"If you know something, then it would be in your best interest to tell someone."

"But I don't know anything. Not really." She sighed heavily as she pushed her hair away from her face. "Look, I just don't want to accuse someone close to me and then it turns out they were innocent." Her face hardened. "I know what that's like, to be accused of something you didn't do. At Daddy's funeral, people were talking about me. Pointing fingers, making little judgments. It was just rumors. Apparently, I was a wild child and out of control. None of it was true. Granted, I wasn't an angel, but I wasn't the heartless monster everyone believed. But I wasn't worried. In fact, I wasn't even worried when the police came and arrested me." She laughed bitterly. "Even then, I stupidly thought everything was going to be okay. I just knew they would capture the killer and I would be set free. Then came the trial. Still, I trusted that I would walk out a free woman. I was innocent, after all. The jury would see that. It came as quite the shock when my lawyer told me that I might spend the rest of my life in prison, and it would be better if I just pled guilty before the case went to the jury. But I told him in no uncertain terms that I was not going to plead guilty to something that I didn't do. However, as we got closer to the end of the trial, he kept pressuring me to take the deal, and in a weak moment, I pled guilty. The lawyers, the cops, everyone let me down. I'll never trust the justice system again." She pursed her lips as she glared down at the table. "Not as long as I live."

"I'm not the law, you know," I pointed out carefully. "I'm just curious. Just who do you suspect?"

Tiffany stubbornly shook her head. "No. I'm not stupid you know. I don't really believe any of you people are here to help me. You want a story. As far as I'm concerned, you reporters are just as dangerous as the cops are. You can destroy someone's life with a couple of keystrokes. I didn't get arrested until that Evan Quincy started publishing those ugly rumors about me. I'm not going to do to someone else, what was done to me." She glared at me reproachfully. "I don't trust you all. You'd sell your own mother for a story."

Knowing for a fact that wasn't true, I snorted. "Have you ever met my mother? People are scared of her. Terrified. I'd have to pay them—" Catching Tiffany's shocked look, I quickly shook my head. "Let's change the subject. When you met Simon outside the Cookie Jar on Valentine's Day, did you happen to see a green and pink striped bag with Dolly's cookies in front of him?"

Tiffany screwed up her face. "I don't think so, but I didn't really pay any attention. Vivian kept calling me. She was in such a weird mood."

"What did she want?"

"She needed me to go to the store and pick up some groceries. She had a date for Valentine's Day and was making ravioli for dinner. That's why I stayed at Simon's that evening. I wanted to give her some privacy. She's been so lonely since Daddy died."

I perked up at this little bit of gossip. "Who is Vivian dating?"

Tiffany bit her lip. "I'm not entirely certain," she said drawing out the last word.

"I'm just going to throw a name out there. It wouldn't be Rich Fairchild would it?"

Tiffany hemmed and hawed for a bit before giving me a very definite, "Umm."

"They seemed pretty chummy at the grand opening."

"Well," she said hesitantly, "to be honest, I don't really know but . . ." She shifted her eyes to the window and the ocean that lay just beyond the glass. The sun was just beginning to set in the distance. "I just really don't know."

I was pretty certain she did know, but decided to change the subject. "Benny was certainly busy that day. Did you know that he and Evan Quincy had words outside of the Cookie Jar? It looked like Evan pushed Benny against the door."

Tiffany gave me a surprised look before smiling slightly. "Good. I hate that man. The things he wrote about me . . . Benny said he'd make him sorry. I thought Benny was just acting tough. Maybe he did still care about me after all."

"Do you know what sort of work Benny did for Vivian?"

"I didn't know he had been working for Vivian. As you've heard, I've been away for a while."

"Yes, I heard." I cleared my throat. "Did Benny have a lot of cash?"

Tiffany looked at me in confusion. "I guess. I don't really know."

I wrote a big fat question mark next to the dollar sign beside Benny's name. "I heard that he and Rich Fairchild fought that day as well."

"Benny was a bit of a hothead."

"What happened?"

"I don't know. I found them in here arguing about respect and money. I heard Rich tell Benny that he had enough of his lies." She held up her hand. "I have no idea what they were talking about. Vivian came in a few seconds later and sent me back to the store for olive oil. That was just an excuse." She pointed to the door next to the stove. "She had a full bottle in the pantry. When I came back from the store, Rich was standing in the driveway sticking a tissue up his nose. I figured Benny must have popped him one. I don't know why. I'm sorry, I really don't know anything more than that. I just dropped off Vivian's olive oil and drove to Simon's place for dinner."

"Was Benny still here?"

"Yeah, but we didn't talk. He was furious about something, but he wouldn't say what. He just told me that he'd explain when I picked him up later that night."

"What time was this?"

Tiffany lifted her eyes to the ceiling. "I think about fifteen minutes before five o'clock." She waved her hand. "Give or take five minutes."

So, just before Benny called me. "Do you know why Benny would want to meet with me?"

"Unfortunately, no I don't. Benny wasn't exactly communicative." She glanced down at my notebook and the notes I had jotted down about Benny Yates. She tapped a manicured fingernail against the paper. "You can add that to your list of vices, along with secretive and annoying." She glanced at her watch and rose to her feet. "Oh, I'm sorry, but I've got to rush." She reached for the purple leather jacket that lay on the stool near the kitchen island. "I promised Vivian I would meet her for lunch in town."

"Just one more question . . . just what was Rich Fairchild doing in Vivian's kitchen on Valentine's Day, while she was getting ready for her big date that night?"

Tiffany's mouth fell open. "Uh . . . I didn't say Rich was in *this* kitchen."

I made a show of looking through my notes. "Yes, I'm afraid, you did."

Tiffany gave me a pained look. "All this is off the record, right? This isn't really something you would print, would you? You can't. I mean, it's over between them now. There's no story anymore."

"Did Vivian tell you that?"

"Please don't say anything. Vivian would kill me if she found out that you got that information from me." Tiffany gripped my arm tightly as she turned worried eyes toward me. "She'd just kill me if she found out that I said anything."

CHAPTER NINE

"No, NOT FRANKIE'S Fish and Chips." I cradled the phone between my shoulder and my ear as I reached for my purse. "Uh, no I can't eat there, either." I glanced over at Hayden who was thumbing through the morning's mail, while trying to pretend that he wasn't listening to every word I was saying. I lowered my voice. "No, that place isn't a good idea, either."

Hayden spared a second to glance my way with a long-suffering sigh.

"The Mad Hatter Tea Room? That's just off the Cheshire Boardwalk, isn't it?" I ran through my mental list of restaurants that I had reviewed recently. Not finding that particular one listed, I said, "Perfect. Give me fifteen minutes. I'll see you there," I said hanging up. I started to stand when I noticed the worried expression on Hayden's face, as he stared down at a small blue box with a pink ribbon.

"What's wrong?" I asked with a chuckle. "Do you have a secret admirer?"

"No, but you do. I don't think this came through the mail and there's no name other than yours on the card." He shook the box lightly near his ear before gazing at it suspiciously.

"Is it ticking?" I asked in amusement.

He shook his head before protectively turning his back to me. I watched as his shoulders suddenly tensed. "What's wrong?"

"Hopefully, you'll enjoy these cookies better than the last batch I made for you." He turned back around. In one hand he held the box, and in the other, a letter on blue stationary. "Eat up, Kat. It's time you get your just desserts."

I stood up and reached for the note, but he jerked it back away from me. "It's bad enough I have my prints on it, we don't need yours, as well." He cleared off a section of Simon's desk and laid the box and letter down.

I glanced down curiously at the box filled with plain, store bought, chocolate chip cookies. "It's a copycat. Some nutcase looking for attention."

"Just the same, we should let the police take a look at it," he said, reaching for the phone. He suddenly smiled. "Just think if it's from the murderer. I bet that'll kill the guys at the Herald."

"Yeah, better them than me," I pointed out as I opened my desk drawer and took out my camera. I snapped a few pictures of the box and letter, as Hayden called the cops. "You know there's no way this is legit," I said when he had ended the call. I waved my hand over the note. "If someone wanted to poison me, why would they warn me first? That letter's practically a neon sign saying, 'these cookies are poisoned.'"

"Crazy people don't always act rationally." He turned toward the coffee pot in the corner of the room. "When the police get here, tell them that we want to know the results of the lab test before anyone else."

"I can't wait for the police." I slung my purse over my shoulder. "You'll have to talk to them."

He turned back around. "What? Why?"

"You don't need me." I patted him on the arm as I brushed past him on my way toward the door. "You're the one who opened the box."

He picked up a chipped coffee cup. "Where are you going?"

I turned back around and smiled. "I have a lunch date."

"Oh, with who?" Hayden asked nonchalantly as he filled his cup with coffee.

"Evan Quincy."

Hayden's eyes flew to mine before cursing slightly, as coffee spilled over the rim of his cup and down his fingers. He quickly placed the pot and cup down on the table before sticking his fingers in his mouth and grimacing. Dragging his fingers back out, he shook them slightly before asking, "Why are you dating Quincy? You have met him, haven't you? I mean, this isn't a blind date, is it? If it is, cancel it. Trust me, you'll thank me later."

"I'm not dating him. This is a business lunch."

Hayden's eyes widened slightly as panic settled in. He closed the distance between us and held up his hands. "Look, I know you hate being our food critic, but trust me, you don't want to work for the Herald. I hear it's horrible over there. They work you to death. You have no say in your story. It's like a factory. And advancing is almost impossible."

As amusing as his sudden concern over my future was, I didn't have time to enjoy it. "I wanted to talk to him about James Wallace's murder. See why he was so convinced Tiffany was the killer. Also, I'm going to try to find out what he and Benny were fighting about the day Benny died."

Hayden visibly relaxed. "Oh. That's good." He glanced down at his burnt fingers. "While you're talking to him, see if you can find out if they're having an opening available and how much they would pay."

"Will do." I reached for the door handle, surprised when Hayden lightly clasped my arm. I looked up into his serious green eyes. "I wouldn't eat or have anything to drink if I were you."

* * *

I pushed open the oddly shaped doors to the Mad Hatter Tea Room and stepped inside. A hostess, dressed in a crushed velvet waistcoat and striped pants with tattered top hat, greeted me and immediately led me into the colorful dining room with its mix and match tables and chairs. She pointed to the trunk of a giant faux redwood tree located in the center of the room. "Mr. Quincy is waiting for you in our private alcove," she said as she led me to a wooden staircase that weaved itself around the trunk. I glanced up as Evan leaned over a branch and waved. Waving back, I made my way up the stairs and to the small, intimate balcony, nestled high above the diners downstairs.

Evan was sitting at a small little table covered by a shabby floral tablecloth, and surrounded by four brightly colored chairs of various sizes, colors, and shapes. A small crystal chandelier hung from a large circular skylight that resembled something off the Millennium Falcon above us, and on the walls were oil paintings of teacups. Naturally hanging upside down.

I sat down just as a waitress lighted the two candles in the center of the table. Another woman with shockingly bright pink hair stood off to the side, nervously gnawing on her bottom lip. As soon as the other girl was done lighting the candles, the pink-haired lady thrust a bright orange menu my way.

I shook my head as I handed it back to her. "Nothing for me, thanks."

Evan made a face. "What? I thought we were having lunch." Evan pointed to the pink lady. "I told Trixie that you were coming. She's the new owner. She was real excited when I told her that Kat Archer from the Gazette was going to be here to test out her food."

Trixie nodded as she looked at me suspiciously. I noticed that her expression changed when she caught my eye. She plastered a friendly smile on her face, which looked more like a tight grimace. "I highly recommend our meatloaf. It is one of our most popular menu items. People absolutely love it."

"That's true," Evan said. "The Herald's food critic raved about it last month. Said it was the best he'd ever had."

"Yes, we love the Herald here bu—but," Trixie stuttered slightly, "we love the Gazette too. In fact, I don't do anything in the mornings until I have a good cup of tea while I read the Gazette. I have had a subscription as long as I can remember. I've recommended it to all my customers." She glanced over at Evan. "And the Herald. Love the Herald." At a loss as to what to say next, she pushed the menu back to me.

I glanced back and forth between Evan and Trixie. Realizing that I was outnumbered, I reluctantly ordered the meatloaf and a soft drink. As soon as Trixie was gone, I glanced at Evan, who was smiling brightly at me. His gold chains glistened in the candle light, projecting little dots onto the walls. I had to admit, it was kind of pretty as I watched them dance about the room. My eyes fell to the dancing pink flamingos in his canary yellow Hawaiian shirt, as he plopped his elbow down on the table and propped his chin up with his hand. "I can't say that I was that surprised when you called me. I knew you would eventually. Especially after we ran into each other during the Cookie Jar's grand opening."

I nodded. Just the opening I needed, but before I could say anything, Evan rambled on. "Yep, I've just been waiting for you to call." He grinned as he ran his hand over his widow's peak. "To be perfectly honest, I was starting to worry, but I figured you were just shy."

I squinted my eyes. *Oh, dear Lord, was he trying to be sexy?*

"I like shy. It's hot." He leaned forward and blinked rapidly, while sticking out his cherry red lips in a pout.

Yep, no doubt about it that was Evan's version of sexy. I wiped off the look of horror that I knew must have been twisting my face. No reason to be rude to a fellow colleague. As my granny used to say, you can trap and kill more beetles with elderberry wine than with a bug zapper. With her admonishment in mind, I leaned back and said, "Get away from me, you hack." Of course, said in the nicest way possible. I looked to the side. *No, that wasn't quite right. Granny didn't talk about beetles.* As I pondered my granny's wise words, my eyes drifted back to the yellow in his shirt. *It was like looking into the sun.* I had to blink rapidly to clear my vision.

Despite, my all too subtle rejection, Evan continued to bat his eyes. Dropping his voice to a lower octave, he whispered, "I think we would be awesome together."

Bees, that's it. Sweet tea and bees. Something about using the sweet tea to lure the bees . . . No wait, not sweet tea; honey. Honey and bees. With a great deal of difficulty, I drew my eyes away from his shirt up to his face.

He licked his red lips as he stared at my cleavage. "I could even put a word in for you at the Herald."

I began to tell him what he could do with that offer, when a sudden thought occurred to me. *Honey and bees involves sex. That can't be right.*

"If you're nice to me." His hand moved a few more inches closer to mine, while my hand instinctively moved a few more inches closer to the butter knife. "There's a journalism conference in Washington next weekend. We could fly out together."

I snapped my fingers. "That's it. Flies. You can buy more honey wine from bar flies faster than you can distill your own vinegar."

Evan pulled back. "What?"

"I don't know. It was something about being sweet to people to get what you wanted. Granny liked to drink on occasion." I waved my hand. Now that mental exercise was over, I could finally get down to business. I picked up his hand, which had somehow fallen to my knee and I laid it on the table. It was just my luck that Evan Quincy was interested in me. *As usual, I have the pick of the litter, unfortunately it's kitty litter in this instance.* "I have no intention of flying anywhere with you. Ever."

He leaned back in a huff. "Then why did you ask me out?"

"This is a professional call. I wanted to talk to you about James Wallace's death. I understand that you covered that case for the Gazette."

He groaned in bitter disappointment. "That's why I'm here? Just go look up my articles. Maybe you'll learn something." He shook a finger at me. "You're paying for lunch."

"Answer my questions and I'll consider it."

He crossed his arms and shook his head. "You think James Wallace's murder is connected to Benny Yate's murder, don't you?"

"The thought crossed my mind. How about yours?" I asked briefly, wondering if he had a mind beneath all that hot air.

"Possibly, but only if Tiffany is the murderer."

"Tiffany has an alibi for Benny's murder."

He snorted. "Alibi's don't work in poisonings. She could have laced the cookies at any time and just waited."

"Why would she kill Benny?"

"She doesn't really have a reason, I guess. The police arrested Dolly, after all."

"I know. I was at the news conference." I leaned back as the waitress handed me my drink and placed a basket of rolls in front of us. As soon as she deposited the drinks, she quickly disappeared down the steps. "Have you heard whether she has made bail, yet?"

"No, not yet."

I took a drink before asking, "So, you think Dolly killed Benny?"

Evan rolled his eyes. "Of course not. Dolly has no motive and I sincerely doubt she wanted to kill you." He leaned forward again. "The only one who wanted Benny dead was Rich Fairchild."

"Why?"

"Because Benny was trying to make trouble for Rich."

"Yeah? How was he going to do that?"

Evan smiled. "You'll just have to read about them in the Herald."

"If it has anything to do with Rich and Vivian's affair, I already know all about it and if that's all you've got, it's not much."

"No, that's not it. That's old news. They'd been secretly seeing each other since before James Wallace died. Everyone knew about that. Dolly knew about that. She caught them in flagrante delicto at a Christmas party a couple of months ago."

I looked at him suspiciously. "Are you sure?"

"Why else did she push Vivian into the fountain at the country club? Trust me, Dolly knew, and has known for years. She just turned a blind eye to it. No, it was something else. I'll let you in on a little secret. Consider it a preview of coming attractions." He leaned forward conspiratorially. "Benny was in love with Vivian. She had him completely wrapped around her finger."

"Really?" Wondering if Vivian was the source of all that money Luke found in his account, I asked, "What exactly did Benny do for Vivian?"

"I don't know, but she must have been paying him top dollar for whatever it was," he said, rubbing his fingers together, "because he was always flush with cash. If you ask me, she and Benny had an arrangement. He took care of her during those times when Rich suddenly realized he had a wife, and would go crawling back to Dolly. I think Rich killed Benny because . . ." He licked his lips. "Well, you'll just have to read the rest in the Herald."

"Yeah? So far, all you have is rumor. Is the Herald anxious to be sued for libel?"

"Don't worry. I'll have stone cold proof soon." He sat back proudly. When I didn't share in his excitement, he added, "All right, I let you in on it. I slipped a little line in the article that we put out about Benny's death this morning. Something to get his killer's attention."

My eyes widened. "What?"

He snapped his mouth shut as our waitress brought our meal. As soon as she had served us and walked back down the stairs, he said in a whisper, "I said that an anonymous source saw Benny's body in the alley holding a note written on blue stationary and ten thousand dollars."

I coughed slightly as I took another drink. "Blue stationary?" I shook my head as I recalled the note Vivian had passed to Rich at the grand opening. "I saw the body. He wasn't holding ten thousand dollars."

"Yeah, that part was a lie. I put that in just to get the killer's attention."

"He also wasn't holding a blue note."

Evan gave me a smug look. "Not when you saw the body he wasn't."

I looked at Evan in surprise. "You saw the body before me?"

Evan shook his head. "No, I wasn't there that night. I got a tip from an anonymous source."

I snorted. "I saw you in the parking lot. You saw me too, and took off in the other direction, remember?"

He turned to the side and glanced over the balcony. "All right. All right. Just keep your voice down." He leaned back toward me and dropped his voice to a whisper. "I got there a half hour before you did. Benny wanted me to meet him behind the Cookie Jar at eleven."

"Did he say why?"

Evan shook his head. "He just told me that he had something to say and that he had called you, and that I had better show up. I got there a few minutes after eleven. The kid was already dead. I was just about to look at the note when I heard someone moving around inside the store."

"Did you see who it was?"

He shook his head.

"You're kidding? You had the murderer right there."

"Hey, the kid was lying dead in the alley. I figured the safest place was behind the fence, so I jumped it. I thought I could spy on whoever was there through one of the slats." He grimaced slightly. "Only problem is, there's a steep ravine behind the fence. By the time, I climbed back up the ravine, the killer and the note was gone. I ran around front to see if I could spot anyone milling around, and that's when I saw you."

"Did you tell the police about the note?"

He grinned. "That new detective came by and questioned me this morning."

"What did you tell him?"

"I told him the truth. That I got that information from a confidential source and that I couldn't divulge their name."

"The truth? Do you have even a passing acquaintance with the truth? You can't claim yourself as a confidential source."

"Why not?"

"Because it's unethical." I shook my head. "Well, has your trick worked?"

"An hour after the article hit the newsstands I received an anonymous note. The killer wants to meet me. He's willing to pay me the ten thousand I had mentioned in the story." Beaming with pride, he clasped my arm. "I'm going to have a one-on-one interview with a killer."

"That's got to be the stupidest thing I've ever heard."

He dropped his hand from my arm. "What? It's just Rich Fairchild. Believe me, I can take him."

"You're going to get yourself killed."

"Oh, don't be ridiculous."

"You're not going alone, are you?"

"If I tell anyone, it might scare him away." He suddenly began to bat his eyes again. "Are you worried about me?"

"Evan, you are dealing with a cold-blooded murderer. At least take someone with you."

"Don't worry. I've got protection. You just keep reading the Herald. In a few days, you'll know who the killer really is."

CHAPTER TEN

"THE COOKIES THAT were delivered here the other day contained traces of strychnine." Luke sat down next to my desk as Rooster weaved through his legs. He bent over and absentmindedly scratched behind the cat's ear.

I glanced over at Hayden's office. Catching his eye through the large glass window that separated his office from the rest of the outer office, I motioned him over. "I still think it was a copycat."

Luke glanced down at Rooster as he shook his head. "Not a copycat. There was—" He did a quick double take. "What happened to your cat?"

Worried that something was wrong, I scooped Rooster up into my arms and looked him over. Finding nothing amiss, I ran my hand down his sleek fur. "He's fine."

Using his thumb and index finger, Luke carefully tilted Rooster's head toward him. "Why is he wearing an eye patch?"

"Cat fight, I assume. Don't you remember seeing him behind the Cookie Jar? You held him for a few minutes."

Luke grinned sheepishly. "Well, I was a bit distracted by the dead body."

I set Rooster back down on the floor. "Not very observant, Detective."

"I call it dedicated," he said with a wink.

St. Valentine's Day Cookie Massacre 99

Hayden sat down on top of Simon's desk. "Have you gotten the test results from the cookies yet?"

Nodding, Luke filled him in on the toxicology report.

"Why are you so certain that it's not a copycat?" I asked.

Luke straightened as Rooster leapt up to Simon's desk and stretched out next to Hayden. "Because underneath the cookies, was Benny's suspended driver's license."

"Suspended?"

"He had a bunch of unpaid parking and speeding tickets. The killer must have taken it out of his wallet when he or she killed him."

"For what reason?"

"Maybe they thought it was a good photo and wanted to admire it for a while." He shrugged. "I don't know. All I know is that it was found underneath those cookies, which means the killer had to have sent you that box."

"Perhaps the killer just wants attention." Hayden ran his hand over his jaw, considering. "Or perhaps, it was some type of trophy."

"It's possible," Luke said. "At this point, we're leaving our options open."

"Really?" I said with a snort. "I thought Chief Waltrip had this case sewn up tight, or does he suspect Dolly sent the box to me from jail."

Luke grinned. "That's the other reason I stopped by. Dolly has been released."

"About time," I said.

"I finally convinced the Chief that only the killer could have sent that box to you, and since she was in jail at the time, it couldn't have been her. She's not out of the woods yet. Waltrip has some officers watching her every move. One mistake and she'll be back in jail."

"I hate to play devil's advocate," Hayden said, "but she could have had someone else drop off the box."

Luke hesitated. "I know, but there was something else."

Hayden leaned forward. "What?"

"Sorry," Luke said with a small smile, "I can't really say at this time."

"Is it about the vial of strychnine poison you guys found when you searched Benny's place?" Hayden asked. "Or was it the syringe you found in his backpack? I hear that tested positive for strychnine, too."

The smile fell from Luke's face, while mine grew broader. *Hayden was definitely full of surprises.*

"How did you get that information?" Luke asked.

"I have sources," Hayden said.

Luke pointed his finger. "I don't want that getting out. We're trying to keep that quiet for now."

Hayden chuckled. "You better talk to your chief then. I sat next to him at the diner down near the courthouse this afternoon. He and his deputy talked about it for quite sometime."

Luke's eyes widened. "You've got to be kidding me. Did anyone else overhear?"

"Oh yeah," Hayden said. "The place was packed with reporters."

"The diner near the courthouse?" I asked. "Isn't that the place that was shut down last month for health violations?" At Hayden's nod, I asked, "Why on earth do you eat there?"

"Oh, I don't eat. I don't think any of the other reporters actually eat there. It just so happens to be Waltrip's favorite restaurant. He has a crush on the waitress."

Shaking his head, Luke leaned his head back and mumbled something unpleasant about our town.

"Why haven't I heard about this?" I complained.

"Because we don't need more than one person covering the diner," Hayden turned back to Luke. "I heard Waltrip say something about suicide."

Luke's face colored. "Now that I've convinced Waltrip that Dolly might be innocent, he's switched gears, and is now floating the theory that Benny killed himself."

I grinned at Hayden. "Maybe he's been talking to Simon." At Luke's confused look, I explained, "That's Simon's theory, as well."

Hayden looked over his shoulder at Simon's empty chair. "Where is Simon by the way?"

I glanced at my watch. Five-thirty. "The Mad Hatter. He's on a date." When Hayden's eyes shifted to Rosie's desk, I shook my head. "I don't know who it was with, but I don't think it was Rosie. Have you ever had their meatloaf? It's excellent, by the way."

Hayden nodded approvingly. "Good. I assume you will be writing up a piece on it at any moment."

"Already did. Check your inbox."

"Well," Luke said slapping his knees and rising to his feet. "As fascinating as this is, I've got things to do."

I wiggled my fingers as he walked out the door.

"So, what are you up to tonight?" Hayden asked me.

At least I assumed he was talking to me. He was actually looking at Rooster when he asked the question, but taking the chance that he was more interested in my nightly activities than a cat's, I said, "Why that's a personal question, Hayden." I tilted my head to the side. "You know I've worked here for three months, and that's the first personal question you've asked me."

Hayden smirked. "Am I being too forward?"

I smiled. "Would you like to be?" My smile grew larger as he turned away. "I thought I would go down to the boardwalk and take a walk. There's this great little ice cream shop down there. You want to come with me?"

He looked around at the virtually empty office and said, "Sure, why not? Maybe I'll get up the nerve to ask a really personal question. Like what's your middle name or something."

"Oh, I'd wait a few months before we talk about names. Maybe years."

He laughed as he followed me out of the office. We continued down the street toward the boardwalk, just half a mile away from the office, chatting aimlessly about nothing in particular until we reached the Snow Cap Ice Cream Shop. I had just sat down at one of the picnic tables out front, when I noticed Evan Quincy pass by, looking like a man on a mission. He glanced over his shoulder nervously as he walked by my table, before continuing down the boardwalk.

Hayden thrust an ice cream cone in my hand. "Here's your mint chocolate ice cream." Licking his vanilla cone, he sat down next to me just as I stood up. "What's wrong?"

"Interested in doing some actual investigating?" I asked before informing him of the trap Evan had set for the murderer.

Eyes wide, Hayden asked, "Do you think he's about to spring it?"

"He definitely looked like he was up to something," I said before taking a few big bites of my ice cream and tossing it into the trash. Normally, I didn't waste food, but it was rather difficult to follow someone while ice cream was running down your fingers.

Hayden stood up and followed suit. We turned and dashed down the boardwalk. It didn't take long until we caught sight of Evan, striding down the boardwalk like he owned it. We spotted him easily in the crowd. He wasn't difficult to miss with his hot pink and green Hawaiian shirt, and lime green walking shorts. We weren't that far from him when he suddenly pivoted around. I ducked behind a hotdog cart and hid, while Hayden threw himself behind a giant palm tree located in front of the Pink Flamingo Inn. I kept my eyes on Hayden, who carefully looked around the tree. After a minute had passed, he finally motioned for me to come over. I stood up and dashed up to him, making sure to keep the palm tree between Evan and me. "Do you think he saw us?"

Hayden shook his head, causing his hair to fall in front of his eyes. Resisting the urge to push it out of his face, I asked, "Where is he going?" We had reached the end of the boardwalk and all that remained were the condemned buildings that had been partially destroyed in a fire that had swept through the boardwalk earlier in the year and a dilapidated pier.

Hayden's eyebrows knitted together. "I have no idea, but he's certainly acting suspicious."

I glanced around Hayden's body. "Okay, he's turned back around. Let's—"

"Kat! Hayden!"

Hayden and I groaned at the same time. I turned around to find Simon and Tiffany staring back at us. They stood a few feet away from us, holding a hotdog and drink in their hands. My eyes widened as I looked from Simon to Tiffany. Talk about opposites attracting. You couldn't get anymore opposite than them. At least as far as fashion went. Tiffany was wearing a beautiful, and probably expensive, blue silk halter-top dress, with princess cut diamond earrings and a sapphire and diamond bracelet, while Simon, on the other hand, was wearing a faded orange t-shirt with ripped cargo pants and purple flip-flops. She looked like she was about to dance the night away. He looked like he was about to pick up cans on the beach. *Someone was going to have to teach Simon how to dress on a date*, I thought, as I shook my head.

"Hey, what are you two doing here?" Simon asked.

I dropped my voice to a whisper. "What are *we* doing here? I thought you were supposed to be at the Mad Hatter."

"We were, but it was packed," Simon said. "So, I thought I would take Tiffany to my favorite dinner place on the boardwalk."

I glanced down at his hotdog and then glanced at the hotdog cart. "Really?"

"Yeah, do you know Tiffany's never eaten out of a hotdog cart before?"

Eyes wide, Tiffany said, "Yep. It's a new experience." She held out her uneaten hot dog. "Do you want a bite?"

I felt Hayden grab my elbow and whisper, "He's getting away," in my ear. "No thanks. Well, you two enjoy." Hayden and I turned around and looked down the boardwalk. Most of the buildings had been torn down after the fire. Only a few remained, and what did, was located behind a yellow police tape that stretched from a palm tree to a post further down the beach. Evan was nowhere to be seen. "He must have ducked into one of the buildings," I said as I followed Hayden to the police tape. He lifted it up slightly as I bent over and slid underneath.

"Hey, you two can't go down there," Simon said from behind me. "It's not safe."

Hayden crossed under the tape. "Don't worry about it. We'll be careful."

"We'll come with you," Simon called out. I glanced back over my shoulder as Simon looked down at Tiffany, who was shaking her head slightly. "Come on, it might be exciting to explore the old boardwalk," he cajoled as he took her hand.

Smiling, she said, "Okay. Sure. Why not."

Hayden and I exchanged a look, while Tiffany and Simon caught up with us. We continued down the beach pausing every few seconds to look into the remnants of the burned out buildings until we came to the last standing structure. We looked out over the large expanse of sand and brush in front of us and the ocean to our left. The only man made thing left to see was the old, battered pier. "Do you think he went down that way?"

"I think we're on a wild goose chase," Hayden said. "Let's just go back. He may have gone around the Pink Flamingo Inn back there while we were hiding behind the palm tree." We both turned to go back the way we came, when suddenly, Tiffany and Simon, who were still facing the pier, gasped. Hayden and I turned around in time to see a man hanging off the edge of the pier. The hot pink in Evan's shirt acted like a bright neon sign drawing our attention toward him, as he struggled to pull himself up. I raised my eyes up past Evan and toward the person in black standing over him.

"That guy in black just hit the other one on the back of the head and pushed him over the railing," Tiffany said in shock. She reached into the white leather purse that was slung over her body, pulled out her phone, and called the police. She quickly began to describe what she was seeing to dispatch, as the figure in black leaned down and appeared to be struggling with Evan's hands. It was difficult to tell, since I was so far away, but from Evan's screams, I was betting the figure wasn't trying to help pull him back up to safety.

Hayden took off toward the pier with me close behind. It seemed to take us forever before we reached the pier and began to run down it. By the time we got to the end, the figure was gone. I spared a few seconds to look into the old, empty, ramshackle bait shop standing at the end of the pier, before dashing up to Hayden who was looking over the edge. Evan was gone.

I glanced over to the beach. Simon stood at the edge of the water. He backed up as the tide washed onto the beach, and I suddenly remembered that he didn't know how to swim. My eyes travelled from Simon to the ocean, surprised to discover Tiffany speedily swimming toward us. I glanced back at Hayden who was stripping off his clothes. "Stay here," he said before jumping into the ocean. I stood at the edge watching anxiously, as first Hayden, and then Tiffany disappeared under the water.

Creak.

I glanced behind me toward the bait shop. The hair on my arms stood on end, as I realized that I didn't really do a very good job searching it a few minutes before. For all I knew, the figure was hiding in there somewhere. I stood up and took a step toward the shop.

A sudden shout from below caught my attention and I turned back around. Hayden and Tiffany were treading water as they held Evan Quincy's body between them. Hayden looked up at me. "Meet us at the beach."

I was just about to answer, when I caught his and Tiffany's horrified expression. Feeling like there was someone behind me, I started to pivot around just as Hayden and Tiffany shouted my name.

CHAPTER ELEVEN

I BLEW OUT my breath as I sat on the hard ER bed, twirling my feet off the edge. I was fine and saw no reason to stick around. The only damage I sustained when I was pushed over the railing was to my arm. It hurt a little, but the doctor assured me that it wasn't fractured.

After I fell, Hayden and I swam back to shore, while Tiffany, the only one of us that had ever been a lifeguard, dragged Evan back to shore. A crowd of onlookers, and a few of my colleagues from the Herald and the local TV crew had already started to gather, tipped off by the police and emergency crew that had arrived at the pier, soon after I took my little swan dive into the ocean. As soon as Tiffany and Hayden deposited Evan on the beach, the paramedics began to work on him. A few seconds later, he was breathing and looking around wildly.

I glanced toward the opposite side of the ER where Evan sat. Deciding that anything was better than just sitting there waiting to be released, I hopped off the bed, wrapped the warm blanket the hospital provided around my shoulders, and made my way across the ER toward Evan's bed.

Evan obviously wasn't the most pleasant of patients. Nurses and doctors cut him a wide berth as they walked about the ER. I couldn't blame them. Evan sat in his dressing gown, with his arms crossed, and a scowl across his face. He glared at everyone around him. Snarling and snapping at anyone within earshot. Only the most fearless dared to approach. Luckily, I had nerves of steel and a charming bedside manner, if I did say so myself. "I told you meeting with the killer was a dumb idea," I said when I finally reached his side.

Evan barely looked up. He just sat on the bed glowering into nothing. I glanced up at the ratted mass of hair which had fallen in front of his face. Little black beads of water from the cheap hair dye he used snaked down his cheeks. I was about to snap my fingers in front of his nose to get his attention, when he finally spoke. "They had the nerve to take my picture while I was passed out with seaweed covering me. I'll tell you this, if that picture ends up on the front-page of my own newspaper, I am quitting. I won't stand for it."

"I wouldn't either." I leaned forward. "So, who tried to kill you?"

"It was the same person who killed Benny Yates. I made plans to meet them on the old pier by the bait shop." His scowl deepened. "I can't believe I was betrayed like that."

"Well, you were meeting with a murderer. They tend not to be the most honorable of people."

"I'm not talking about the killer. I'm talking about my own co-workers. I wake up on the beach with paramedics bending over me, and they are hovering around snapping pictures."

"Would you relax, they probably won't even print the pictures."

"Oh, trust me, they will. They will rue the day they messed with Evan Quincy."

"You should be happy you're alive. If Hayden and Tiffany hadn't jumped in to save you—"

He shook his head hard enough for his water logged hair to whip around, spraying little black droplets of water all over the hospital's blanket, and my light blue Capri pants. I scooted back to avoid any more damage from Evan's hair dye.

"The only reason I am alive is because the killer realized I didn't know what was on that blue stationary."

"Yeah, how did he know that?"

"Because I was screaming that I didn't know. Luckily, whoever it was, finally believed me and ran off. I would have climbed back up myself if that stupid railing hadn't given away. I must have hit my head on it on the way down."

"Could you tell anything about the person? Their sex, height, weight. Anything at all?"

"They were a horrible dresser."

"That's helpful."

"Hey, the first time I saw them, I was hanging from the pier. It was kind of hard to get a good look at their body."

"What about hair or eye color?"

"They had grey hair, I think. I'm pretty sure it was a wig. I don't know about eye color. It was really hard to tell, since a Halloween mask covered their entire face. I think it might have been a woman. The killer's shoulders weren't that wide and had hands that were rather small." He nodded vigorously. "Yeah, now that I think about it, I'm pretty sure it was a woman who attacked me."

"Well, I guess that narrows it down some."

He threw up his hands. "No it doesn't. None of it makes any sense. I thought for sure I was about to meet Rich Fairchild. I know he hated the kid."

"From what I understand, lots of people hated Benny, not just Rich."

Evan's eyes narrowed. "What do you mean by that?"

"I saw you two fighting the day he died."

"I didn't kill him. If I wanted him dead, I would have strangled him with my bare hands." He reached out his arms and made a choking motion with his clenched hands. "I wouldn't have poisoned him."

"Why were you so angry with him?"

"Because I found out the snake was using me. Can you believe it? He was feeding me misinformation. The ungrateful moron. I'm the one who got him that job at the courthouse."

I sat down next to his bed. "What happened?"

"Last month, I told Benny that I was being blackmailed, and that I suspected that it was someone from the courthouse. Since he worked there, I figured he'd be just the guy to nose around."

My eyes widened. "Blackmail?"

"The day before Benny died, he told me that I wasn't being blackmailed by anyone at the courthouse. He told me that it was Rich that was blackmailing me, and that he had proof."

I leaned forward eagerly. "Really? Why are you being blackmailed?"

Evan made a face. "I wasn't. It was all a lie. See, I began to get suspicious that Benny was using me to get back at people that he was angry with by feeding me false information. So, I set a little test for him. I had heard that he hated another clerk at the courthouse, and wanted to see if he would try to point the finger at her. But, apparently, he hated Rich more. He was jealous of Rich Fairchild and wanted to get him into trouble. He probably thought that if Rich went away, he could have Vivian all to himself. By the time Benny was done, you would have thought that Rich was running a blackmailing scheme from coast to coast." Evan's face turned purple and his hands clenched again. "Benny lied to me. My reputation hangs on some of the things he told me. Of course, I was angry, but *I'm* not the one who killed him. Rich has just as much reason. He was pretty furious when I called him right before Dolly's grand opening and told him what Benny had said. He said that he was going to kill the kid."

"So, you think that Benny tried to implicate Rich in a crime because he was in love with Vivian and that Rich decided he had enough and killed him?"

Evan looked around before leaning closer. "That's exactly what I thought. See, Benny had been after Vivian ever since her husband died. Probably even before that. I don't think he was ever interested in Tiffany. He was just using her to get close to her step-mom or maybe the Wallace fortune. After Wallace died, and Tiffany went away, he moved in on Vivian. He was always hanging around her house. He'd do anything for her. I think she liked his attention, but I think she liked making Rich jealous more. See that was Benny's problem. Vivian never really cared about him. She's in love with Rich Fairchild. Has been ever since he blew into town. She just used Benny. She use to call him her go-to boy." Evan leaned back against the pillow, puffed out his chest, and smoothed his hair back. "There was a time when Vivian looked my way. Unfortunately, it just wasn't meant to be. I just can't be tied down."

I rolled my eyes. "Let's try to focus here, Romeo." My mind drifted back to James Wallace's murder. "You said that Benny has been after Vivian ever since James Wallace died. Perhaps even before. He didn't happen to feed you information about Tiffany Wallace, did he?" I watched as Evan shifted uncomfortably on the bed. "Was he your source?"

Evan shrugged. "It was such a long time ago. He might have mentioned a few things." He held his finger up.

"Look, that was completely on the up and up. She killed James Wallace."

"According to Benny?"

Evan nodded. "Yes—I mean, well, not just him. Everyone thought that Tiffany murdered her father. Everyone."

Suddenly, the hanging drape separating Evan from the other patients flew opened to reveal a very angry Tiffany Wallace. She didn't look much better or happier than Evan did with her hair dripping down her face, and a bandage across her nose. Her eyes had even started to blacken where my arm had inadvertently struck her on my way down. Her upper lip curled up in distaste. "Just what do I have to do to prove to you that I am innocent? I saved your life. Doesn't that count for anything?"

"I said thank you," Evan snapped.

Tiffany tried jerking the curtain back, but being a curtain, it didn't have the same effect as a good door slam. Patting Evan on the arm, I stood up and dashed around the bed. I pulled the curtain to the side and stuck my head through the opening, surprised to find Vivian Wallace lying in the bed with her arm thrown over her eyes. Tiffany sat on the other side of the bed looking like she swallowed a lemon.

"Vivian, what happened?" I asked in concern.

Vivian raised her arm just enough to look at me and cried out, "I'm a dead woman." She dropped her arm across her eyes and moaned dramatically.

I glanced over at Tiffany who just rolled her eyes. "She's fine."

"No, I'm not," moaned the woman from the bed. She threw out her other hand. "Tiffany, sweetheart, please find the doctor and tell him that I need to see him."

Sighing heavily, Tiffany stood up and pushed aside the curtain.

"Are you sick?" I asked.

Vivian dropped her arm to her side. "I'm next."

I sat down in the seat Tiffany had just vacated as Vivian pushed herself in a semi sitting position. I looked at her in concern. I'd never seen the woman looking so bedraggled before. Her hair, which had always been styled and coiffed to an inch of its life, now lay limply around her shoulders. Even her makeup looked hastily done. Heavy mascara smudges appeared above and beneath her eyes, and her lipstick was smeared across her lips.

Vivian Wallace was definitely not herself. She clutched at my arm. "I can trust you, can't I? You're Sarah's daughter. I remember you. You used to stay at my house when you were little. Do you remember that?"

She relaxed when I said I did, only to tense back up again a few seconds later. "Those cookies Benny ate were meant for me."

"What makes you think that?"

"The police won't believe me. I've called them a dozen times since Benny's death, but they just think I'm paranoid. Even that tall good-looking one." Her fingernails dug painfully into my arm and I bit my lip to keep from gasping. I placed my hand over hers and attempted to pry her fingers away, surprised when she simply moved her hand to my other wrist. "Please, you must help me. They're going to kill me. I just know it. No one will believe me. I only eat or drink things that I buy for myself, but I'm so afraid I'm going to make a mistake."

I finally pried her hands loose and patted her arm. "Who do you think is trying to kill you?"

She made a face as though the answer was obvious. "Rich and Dolly, of course," she said in a shrill tone.

Her lover and his wife? "But I thought you and he—"

She waved her hand dismissively. "No, that's been over for days."

"That long?"

She looked at me as though I was an idiot. "Yeah, of course. I dropped him the moment I found out that he brought me poisoned cookies for dessert."

"When did he do that?"

"Valentine's Day. The night Benny died. Aren't you paying attention? Rich came over to my house for Valentine's Day. We were going to have a nice, romantic dinner, while Dolly was at her grand opening gala," she said derisively. "It was his turn to bring the dessert. And what do you think he brought me?"

"Poisoned cookies?"

"Yes. If Benny hadn't taken them . . . I was so angry when I found out he just left with them, but now . . ." She clutched at her neck. "If that poor boy hadn't taken them away with him when he left, I'd be dead right now."

"I'm surprised that Benny ate the cookies at all."

"Why?"

"They were coffee flavored. Tiffany said he hated anything with coffee, that it made him sick."

Vivian shook her head. "I remember that. He was lying. She made him a mocha flavored cake for his birthday one year." She made a face and dropped her voice to a whisper. "It wasn't good. He just said that so he wouldn't have to eat anymore. Tiffany's sweet, but she is an awful cook. Simply dreadful. If I wasn't here to cook for her, I think the girl would probably starve. Thank God, he took those cookies." The corners of her mouth lifted slightly. "Stupid boy. He was angry with me. That's why he stole them from my kitchen counter."

"Why was he angry?"

"He asked me to marry him months ago. I refused, of course. He was a nice boy, but he wasn't really my type." She clutched my arm again. "I want you to know that I let him down gently. We were still good friends. Benny was always such a help to me. It's just that he was so very young, and I could never be sure if it was my money or me that he was interested in. Anyway, after Rich and I had our fight on Valentine's Day, Benny took the opportunity to ask me to marry him again, and I said no. Again." Her eyes narrowed. "That's when he told me that I'd be sorry."

"What do you think he meant by that?" I asked dragging my arm away from her clawing fingernails once again.

She raised her hand to her face. "I really don't know. Benny was so unpredictable at times. He had such a temper."

"Well, it was a good thing he took the cookies before you could eat one."

"But I did." She reached out and grabbed my arm once again. Her voice dropped to the barest whisper. "I ate one cookie."

"But you couldn't have." I forcefully pulled her hand away from my arm once again and laid it on her lap where it twitched nervously. "You would have died if you had eaten any."

"I'm telling you that I did," she snapped.

I reached into my purse, which was still slung across my body, and pulled out my notebook. I groaned in frustration as my fingers encountered a soggy wet mess. I brought it out anyway. "Do you remember how many were in the bag before you took one?"

"Three, I think. Why?"

I carefully pulled apart the pages, revealing nothing but page after page of smeared blue ink. Realizing the notebook was destroyed, I dropped it back into my purse. Luckily, not all was lost. I had transcribed my notes every time I had gone back to the office, which meant that I still had another copy on my computer. Unfortunately, that meant I was going to have to operate by memory for the time being. "There had been four in the bag originally. My co-worker ate one of the cookies and you ate the other. Obviously, neither one had been poisoned. And we know that Benny ate two which were poisoned. So, the strychnine had to have been introduced sometime after you ate the second cookie."

"I wouldn't be surprised. I ran upstairs for a few seconds to change for dinner, and when I came back, I found Rich holding one of the cookies." She looked at me meaningfully as she reached for my arm. "Don't you see? That's when he put the poison in the cookies."

I sat back more to evade her hands than for any other reason. If Vivian was telling the truth, then the killer had to have poisoned the cookies in her kitchen. The syringe was found in Benny's backpack, but the killer could have planted it there, perhaps to throw suspicion on Benny. *Surely, Benny didn't poison the cookies himself. If he had, he wouldn't have eaten any of them.* "But why would Rich want to kill you?"

"I don't know, but he threatened me when I ran into him at the Cookie Jar later that night."

"You both were at the Cookie Jar? What time was that?"

"A little after ten-thirty." She hiccupped. "He told me that he didn't love me. His eyes. You should have seen his eyes. He was so cold. He threw me out of the store and told me that if I ever came back that I'd regret it."

"That's it?"

Vivian's face twisted into a ugly scowl. "I'm sure Dolly put him up to it. He's devoted to her."

"He has a strange way of showing it."

"He'd do anything for her. I begged him to leave her, but he always refused." She swiped at her eyes. "He said that he loved her. I finally had enough. Here I made a wonderful dinner for him, and all he could talk about was how Benny ruined Dolly's big day. I just don't understand. Look at me. I'm beautiful and I have more money than she does. Why would he want to stay with her over me? He obviously enjoys my company. Why?"

I stared at the hysterical, bedraggled woman in front of me. "I have no idea. You're obviously a catch." Still, unwilling to give up my idea that James and Benny's deaths were connected, I said, "Let's pretend for a moment that you weren't the intended target. Can you think of anyone who would have wanted both James Wallace and Benny Yates dead?"

Vivian hissed at me in annoyance. "This doesn't have anything to do with James. Rich wasn't even in town when James died." She sneered. "He supposedly was on his second honeymoon with Dolly."

"It's rather coincidental that he and Dolly would be using the same method that killed your husband."

"They're probably hoping that the police will blame Tiffany again."

"Who inherits from you if you died?"

"Rich," she said softly. "He knew he was my beneficiary. We had talked about it. I called my attorney and had him change the will yesterday. I've left everything to my six sisters and three brothers."

"No one else?" I asked, thinking of Tiffany. If she was truly innocent as I suspected, it seemed rather unfair that she wouldn't inherit anything of her father's estate.

Vivian must have read my mind. Her face reddened as she glanced past me. Pressing a hand to her face, she said, "I'm a horrible person. It's really Tiffany's money. The only reason she didn't inherit the vast majority of it, was because she pled guilty to killing her father. The poor girl was innocent." She took a deep breath. "I'll call my attorney as soon as I leave here and put some money in trust for her. I'm sure my siblings would be willing to part with a small amount."

"Yeah, I'm sure that's what her father would have wanted."

Vivian's face crumpled. "You know those cookies that you received the other day? The police came to talk to me about them. That was my box the killer used. I had dozens of those boxes in my closet. I used to use them in my catering company. Those cookies that they sent to you were a warning to me that I was next."

"A warning for you?"

"Yes, absolutely." She swiped at her eyes, smudging the dark black mascara across her cheeks. "They want me dead. I can feel it." She clutched at her throat. "They're closing in on me."

"So, Benny's death and my threat were about you?"

"Yes, everything is about me. Don't you see?" She placed her hand against her neck and arched her back slightly.

I leaned back as I watched her contort her body. "I think I'm beginning to."

Vivian nervously tugged on her ear before jerking her hand through her hair.

"Are you okay?"

"Do I look okay?" Vivian snapped. "Of course, I'm not okay. I just told you my ex-lover or his wife, or maybe both of them are trying to kill me. Would you be okay?"

She closed her eyes and took a deep breath. "I'm sorry. I don't know what's happened to my manners. I'm not usually this abrupt. I didn't get any sleep last night. I think I must have tossed and turned all night." She reached up, clasped her hand against the back of her neck, and stretched. "When I finally fell asleep, it was out in my living room. I can barely move today."

"Are you sure that's it?" I asked slowly. "Maybe you should ask the doctor to take a blood test."

She turned frightened eyes to me. "Why? I just slept wrong, is all."

I bit my lip. "It's just you're exhibiting some of the signs of strychnine poisoning. Paranoia, muscle spasms. Arching your back. They're all signs." I immediately regretted my words as soon as they left my mouth. No sooner had I mentioned the word strychnine, than Vivian began to moan and groan. She caused such a ruckus that the nurses rushed forward and summarily ordered me back to my bed.

CHAPTER TWELVE

I SHUT THE door to my apartment and made my way down to the business district. There was a nice breeze coming off the ocean nearby, and I decided to take a walk down to the Cookie Jar, which had just reopened. It had been a few days since the "Terror on the Pier," or so my headline had proclaimed, and after a nice long weekend relaxing out on the beach and sleeping in, I decided to pick back up on my investigation. I hadn't been completely unproductive. Sunday morning at church, I had reconnected with one of my most reliable confidential sources, who just so happened to be a childhood friend of both Dolly Fairchild and Vivian Wallace. My source, who I liked to call Mom, managed to give me an inside view into their sordid history. And sordid it was.

I had been under the impression that Dolly and Vivian's friendship had ended due to a bad business deal, but the truth was it ended because of Rich Fairchild, a former tennis pro who blew into town one summer ten years ago and immediately began offering his services to some of the wealthy and lonely Hatter's Cove ladies.

It wasn't long until Vivian Matthews, as she had been known back then, latched onto him. She seemed determined to make him her own. However, it was Dolly who eventually won our tennis pro's fair heart with her sweet nature.

My mother was sure it had nothing to do with the money Dolly had made from her successful business ventures. Oh no, absolutely not, she said to me with a roll of her eyes.

Compared to Dolly's net worth, poor Vivian had very little to offer him. She was on a downward spiral at the time. She had just invested every dime she had in a catering business that was failing.

In any event, for whatever reason, Rich chose Dolly. They were extremely happy—at first. Mom truly believed that Rich had grown to love Dolly. Everyone did. However, as Dolly's business grew, she began to spend more time away from home, leaving Rich to fend for himself. With so much free time and so very little companionship from his new wife, he developed a wandering eye.

Meanwhile, Vivian nursed her heartbreak by marrying the richest man in town, James Wallace. The Wallace marriage was more of convenience than love. They apparently had an understanding. She would help him with the house, hang on his arm during business parties, and be somewhat of a friend to his teenage daughter, while he in return, would provide her with as much material goods as she desired. What she did on her own time was none of his business, and as long as she was discreet and didn't embarrass him, he would turn a blind eye to it all. So, not long after the wedding, Vivian set about trying to—discreetly—woo Rich back into her arms. It didn't take long before they were secretly together once again.

But alas, their love wasn't meant to be. Mom wasn't quite certain as to exactly why the two parted ways a few years later but she was fairly certain that they had called an end to their affair just before James Wallace died. As far as Mom knew, they had remained nothing more than friends, until a few months ago when Dolly decided what fun it would be to have her very own bakery.

With that bit of history percolating in my mind, I opened the door to the Cookie Jar to find Dolly standing behind the counter.

As soon as she saw me, she rushed forward and greeted me as if she hadn't seen me in years. "Oh, Kitty Kat, this whole thing is just so dreadful. I can't believe someone would use my cookies to kill Benny." She ran her hand over my hair. "I'm just so glad that you didn't eat any."

"So am I."

"Well, don't you worry. I've been making another batch." She pushed me into a chair. "Now, you just sit here. I will be right back." She pinched my cheek before running into the back of the store. A few minutes later, Rich appeared at the door. He took one look at me and froze. I called his name before he could duck back into the back room, and pushed the chair across from me out with my foot. "Join me," I said loudly.

Dolly peered over his shoulder. She pushed him aside with her hip and deftly maneuvered around him. In her hands was a tray filled with chocolate candies and a cup and saucer. Proudly, like a jeweler displaying the crown jewels, she carefully and with great solemnity, sat the tray down in front of me. "Now this is just a snack, while I bake those cookies for you. Here, I want your opinion on each and every one of them," she said as she shoved a chocolate truffle in my mouth. "And this," she said with a beatific look on her face, "is my world famous hot chocolate." She sat the pink china cup and saucer down in front of me, taking great care not to spill a drop of the obviously precious liquid.

"It's ninety degrees outside," I protested over a mouthful of chocolate.

Dolly smiled brightly. "Hot chocolate doesn't know seasons. You can have it any time of year," she assured me happily.

Rich Fairchild looked at me nervously. His bright blue eyes travelled over my head to the front door. "Dolly, I'm going to go down to the boardwalk. There's something I need to . . . to . . ." His handsome face twisted in a grimace as his eyebrows drew down in thought. "...get something," he ended helplessly. "At the store."

I shook my head. "No, Rich, please sit with me." I twisted my features into a pout as I gazed up at the two of them. "I absolutely hate eating alone."

He looked ready to protest, but luckily, I had Dolly on my side. "Oh, of course, he will," Dolly said as she shoved her husband into a chair. "He'd be happy to keep you company while I go finish my cookies." She glanced back my way and pointedly looked at the hot chocolate. Sighing, I picked up the cup and took a drink. When she was finally satisfied that I drank and ate enough of her concoctions, she hustled back into the back room, practically trilling as she went. *It has to be the chocolate that keeps her so hyper*, I thought, as I watched her go. I glanced back at Rich. "How are you doing, Rich?"

Rich snorted. "What do you want, Kat?"

"I just want to talk."

He crossed his arms. "Sure you do."

"I could always talk to Dolly. I don't think she'd like what I'd say though." Truth was, I did not intend to talk to Dolly, especially about her husband's affairs, but I had to say something to encourage him to open up. According to Mom, Dolly knew all about the affair, but refused to speak about it with anyone, not even her closest friends. So, if she chose to pretend that it wasn't happening, I wasn't going to be the one to force her to confront the issue. With any luck, her husband wouldn't be too eager to have me to do it, either.

He glanced over his shoulder nervously before leaning forward. He dropped his voice to a whisper. "What do you want to know?"

I followed his lead and leaned forward. For ten minutes, we discussed everything that happened from the morning of the grand opening to when he arrived at Vivian's house that afternoon. I didn't learn any new bombshells, but I was able to confirm a few things Evan, Tiffany, Vivian, and Simon had reported to me. That is right up until we got to the part about who took the cookies to Vivian's house.

Rich looked confused. "I didn't bring any dessert."

"Vivian said you brought her some of Dolly's cookies. They were in a pink and green striped bag."

He rubbed his hand against his forehead. "No, they were already on her kitchen table when I got there."

I crossed my arms, not quite sure that I believed him. "What were you doing there that night?"

"It was Valentine's Day, and Vivian thought I would want to spend it with her." His face turned cold. "She passed me a note during the grand opening demanding my presence at her house that night."

I raised my eyebrow. "Wouldn't Dolly notice you were gone?"

Rich shook his head. "Dolly was planning to stay here until closing. Vivian thought that meant I'd have plenty of time to be with her. She planned a romantic dinner for just the two of us, but I had different plans. Truth is that, I didn't go to her house for dinner." His eyes flashed angrily. "I went to tell her that we were through. I just couldn't take it anymore. She was so determined to hurt Dolly, it just made me sick. She wanted me to steal Dolly's new recipe and give it to her, but I wouldn't do it."

"Why would she want that? I saw Vivian at the grand opening. It didn't really seem like she cared for Dolly's cookies."

"You mean when she threw it in the trash? Yeah, I saw that, too. That was just for show. She knew they were good."

I shook my head. "You're losing me."

"Vivian was trying to figure out what was in Dolly's new cookies. I made the mistake of telling her how good they were, and that they would probably be our best seller after Dolly's done testing it out. As soon as Vivian heard that, she had her heart set on stealing it and presenting it as her own. She's planning on opening her own bakery across from the Cookie Jar. She begged me to get the recipe, but I refused."

"What's so special about those cookies?"

Rich made a disgusted face. "It's not about the cookies. It's about competition. Those two have been competing since they were children, and Vivian's desperate to prove that she's better than Dolly. Despite her looks, she is very insecure. She's jealous of Dolly's success and it killed her when Dolly's business took off and her business failed. Absolutely destroyed her. She's been obsessed with opening a new business and proving that she's better than Dolly ever since. She didn't care about me. She never cared about me. She just wanted to hurt Dolly. So, when I wouldn't give her the recipe, she stole that bag of cookies. She was hoping that if she could figure out the recipe, she could use it to launch her new venture."

"I'm surprised you wouldn't just give her the recipe if it was that important to her."

Rich looked hurt "I know what you think of me. I wouldn't do that to Dolly. I couldn't do that. Dolly keeps her recipes locked away. I couldn't steal them even if I wanted to."

"Did Benny have access to the recipe?"

"Oh no. Dolly is very careful about her business. I love her, but she doesn't trust anyone. At least not about her business. She's very protective about her brand."

"And you're sure the cookies were already there when you got to Vivian's?"

He made a face. "Positive. I don't know how she got her hands on them, but she did. Benny probably stole them." His eyes narrowed suspiciously. "Why are you so concerned about those cookies?"

"Because, I believe they were poisoned."

Rich paled. "You're kidding?" He looked down at the table. "I almost ate one when I was at Vivian's."

"Why didn't you?"

"Vivian yanked it out my hand. She said she needed all of them to test, and that I was eating her samples. I told Vivian that she was losing her mind and that's when we started to fight. I was just about to leave when Benny showed up, and then we got into it."

"I guess you were pretty angry that Benny accused you of blackmailing Evan."

"Evan tell you about that?" At my nod, he said, "I was furious. We even came to blows, but I swear to you, I did not kill Benny or poison those cookies."

"What did you do when you left Vivian's house?"

"I came back here to the Cookie Jar to talk to Dolly. She was still cleaning up the mess Benny made when he attacked Simon. I finally convinced her to go home and relax. We ended up having a nice Valentine's Day dinner at home." His voice softened. "It was our first one in a long time. We ended up talking for hours."

"And?"

"And what?"

"You didn't meet Vivian here at the store that night?"

Rich made a face. "Yeah, okay, I ran into Vivian a few hours later."

"What were you doing here?"

"Cleaning up. I felt so bad for Dolly. She had planned everything down to the last second, and the fight just completely ruined her day. I just wanted to do something nice for her. So after she went to bed, I came back here." His eyes turned hard again and he pursed his lips together into a tight line. "Vivian showed up twenty minutes later. I told her to go home, but she demanded that I let her inside. She said that Benny was in there and that she had to speak to him. She was acting manic and running around talking to herself. She searched the entire store, even the closet. She was convinced he was in there and hiding from her."

"Did she say why she wanted to see Benny?"

Rich looked uncomfortable. "All she would say is that he had threatened her, and that she wasn't going to let him get away with it. She was just acting so strange that I finally threw her out and told her to go home. I finished cleaning up and went home."

I took a deep breath as a picture of the day's events started to take hold in my mind. On a hunch, I asked, "Did you take the trash out?"

Rich looked surprised. "Um, no. I just went home."

"Really? You cleaned up, but you didn't drag out all the broken boxes, ripped ribbon, and torn Valentine decorations, and place them by the trash?"

He cleared his throat. "Okay, yes. I took the trash out but—"

"And saw Benny's corpse lying in the alley," I finished for him. "Don't bother denying it. I have a witness who saw Benny's body shortly after eleven. If you took out the trash you must have seen it as well . . . or was Benny still alive at the time?"

He smashed his lips together and sat silently for a few seconds, before glancing over his shoulder nervously. "I didn't kill him. I didn't even see him until I dropped the garbage into the trash."

"What time was that?"

"About eleven o'clock."

"And you didn't call the police?"

"I didn't know what to do. I guess I panicked. I just closed up and went home."

"Is that all you did? My understanding is that Benny had a piece of paper in his hand."

Rich shook his head. "I don't know anything about it."

"I think you do." I reached into my purse and dragged out my new notebook. I flipped through the pages until I found the print out of my notes concerning Evan's nighttime escapade behind the fence on Valentine's Day. "I have a witness that stumbled on the body at about eleven o'clock, just a few seconds before you took out the trash, in fact, and according to the witness, Benny was holding a note on blue stationary in his hand, but when the witness returned a few minutes later, the note was gone."

Fear, raw unadulterated fear, spread across his handsome face. "I don't know what you're talking about. I didn't see any note."

I snapped my notebook shut. *Time to try a different tactic.* "Look, I don't think you killed Benny, but you are in a lot of trouble. You admitted to fighting with him earlier in the day. I have a witness that can put you at Vivian's house with the poisoned cookies. Now you tell me you were at the store and saw the dead body, but didn't call the police."

"What should I do?" he asked in an anguished voice.

"Tell me the truth. Did you see the note?"

"Yeah, okay," he said softly as his eyes welled up with tears. "I recognized the note paper and picked it up."

"What do you mean you recognized the paper?"

"Vivian has this fancy stationary in her kitchen that she jots notes on. I knew it was hers as soon as I saw it. I picked it up and stuck it in my pocket."

"Why?"

"Because I still cared for Vivian," he said quietly. "I didn't love her. At least, not like I loved Dolly, but I didn't want her to go to jail. Not over someone like Benny."

"What did the note say?"

"It was a confession of sorts. Benny had written down a list of events surrounding James Wallace's death. According to Benny's note, Vivian killed her husband, and then covered it up by letting her stepdaughter take the fall. I still can't believe that she would frame Tiffany. I thought that she liked the girl. I thought she cared for her . . . or as much as Vivian is capable of caring for anyone. It was funny. She was always so certain that Tiffany was innocent. No matter what evidence came out implicating Tiffany, Vivian never waivered." His laugh came out strangled, "I guess we know why now."

So, Vivian Wallace killed her husband. I tapped my pen against the table. *It's possible. According to Mom, she didn't love the man, but could she have killed him?* I shook my head as I looked across the table at the distraught man in front of me. *Benny wasn't a very reliable source, but neither was Rich.*

"What did you do with the note?"

"I burnt it." He looked up sadly.

"Because you didn't want Vivian to go to jail?"

He laughed bitterly. "As you might have guessed, I'm not that noble. I was also afraid that if she were blamed, they would accuse me, too. Apparently, James decided to divorce Vivian because of our affair."

I lifted my hand. "Wait. It was my understanding that if Vivian was discreet then he didn't really care."

"That's was true for a while, but I guess it started to get to him. Benny wrote that the old guy became worried that people were laughing at him behind his back. They weren't. Only a handful of people knew about Vivian and me."

"How did she react?"

"Not well, I'm sure. She may not have loved James, but she did love being Mrs. Wallace and all the money and prestige that came with it. I had no idea until I saw that note that he had threatened her with divorce. I just remember her being so sad. I met with Vivian the morning before Tiffany's birthday. She wouldn't tell me what was wrong. She just said that it was over between us and that she didn't want to see me anymore. I was shocked but relieved, too. I just felt so much freedom when she called it off. I went home to Dolly and decided to make things right. We flew to Vegas and renewed our wedding vows that night and the next day, we flew to Europe for a second honeymoon. We didn't find out about James until we returned a week later."

"How romantic," I said. "Well, that gives you quite the nice alibi for James Wallace's murder. That is, if you can prove what you just told me."

"Of course, I can prove it. You can see our wedding license from Vegas and the pictures from our honeymoon. Look, I didn't kill Benny or James. I had nothing to do with either death, and I swear I knew nothing about it. Vivian killed them, not me. She's lost her mind. She even tried to kill Evan the other day."

"How do you know it was her on the pier?"

He laid his face into his hands. "It was all my fault. I should have kept my mouth shut." He lifted his head up. "When I saw the note and what it said, I confronted Vivian about it. She denied everything, but didn't calm down until I told her that I had destroyed it. Then when I saw Evan's article on Benny, I went to her and showed her what he had written about the murder. I knew that Benny hadn't had any money on him when he died, and knowing Evan as well as I did, I figured he was just trying to set a trap for Benny's killer. I went to Vivian to warn her. I told her it was probably a trick and not to fall for it. She began freaking out." His brow furrowed. "She just kept saying that we had to stop him. Then the next thing I heard was that someone tried to kill Evan on the old pier. It had to have been her. She needs help. She's getting worse."

We leaned away from each other as Dolly came back out of the store carrying a plate of cookies. She took one look at what was left of the desserts and tut-tutted. "You haven't touched a thing," she said before shoving one of the best tasting cookies I have ever eaten in my life into my mouth.

CHAPTER THIRTEEN

I RAN TO the office closet and pulled out a rolling chalkboard that we kept in storage. It used to contain information on assignments and such, but since everyone had electronic calendars that could do the same thing, we mainly kept it around for nostalgia. I rolled it in front of Hayden and stepped next to it, doing my best impersonation of Vanna White.

"Very impressive," he said dryly. "I can't read a word of it, but it looks great. What is it?"

"It's a list of suspects." I pointed toward the board. "We have five suspects for Benny's death. Dolly, Rich, Evan, Tiffany, and Vivian. I think we can eliminate Dolly." I ran a line through Dolly's name. "One, Dolly's a shrewd businesswoman. She's not going to use her own cookies to poison someone. And two, I'm pretty confident the poison was injected into the cookies at Vivian's house, and we know from speaking to Rich that Dolly spent the rest of the evening either at the Cookie Jar, or her house, and no one mentioned seeing her at Vivian's anytime that day. Not to mention the box that was sent here showed up while she was in jail. Besides, if she wanted to poison me she could have easily done it a couple of hours ago." My mouth began to involuntary water as I remembered the taste of those cookies. "Oh, by the way, I'll be submitting an article about Dolly's new recipe soon. She's asked me to wait a few weeks before publishing it. She's still playing with the ingredients."

Hayden seemed less than interested. He peered at the board and squinted his eyes. "You should type everything. Your penmanship is horrible."

I glanced back at the board. "I can read it."

"Well, you can rule out Evan, too. No one saw him at Vivian's either, and we were there when the killer attacked him."

I ran a line through his name. "I agree." I stood back and surveyed my board. "That leaves Vivian, Rich, and Tiffany."

"And Tiffany was with us when Evan was attacked, so that brings us down to Vivian and Rich. What did Rich say to you when you interviewed him?"

I quickly filled him in on what I had learned. "Get this. After I spoke to Rich, I called Luke and told him what I discovered, and I made him promise to compare notes with me as soon as he spoke to Rich."

"And?"

"Luke just called a few minutes ago. They can't find Rich, and Dolly doesn't have any idea where he is. He's been missing ever since I spoke to him earlier today."

"Do you think Rich was telling the truth?"

"I don't know what to think. Rich tells a good story, but that was all that it was. Without the note, no one can prove or disprove what it said. For all we know, he could be lying." I shook my head. "Everything he said makes sense, though. Vivian inherited a huge fortune after James Wallace died and Tiffany was eliminated as a beneficiary. If James Wallace threatened to divorce her, I could see her lashing out."

Hayden bit his lip. "Not everything makes sense. I remember Tiffany Wallace's trial. Based on Tiffany's own testimony, there was no way Vivian could have killed James Wallace."

"Why?" I dropped down in my chair and gazed up at him.

"James Wallace's body was found in his office at the country club at about a quarter after midnight by the night watchman. Vivian testified that she never left the house that night. So, how could she have poisoned him?"

"Maybe she poisoned the liquor at some other time and just waited for him to take a drink."

"They only found poison in his glass, not the decanter, which meant someone had poisoned his drink there."

I sat back, propped my feet up on my desk and closed my eyes. A few seconds later, I felt a small weight jump on my legs. I glanced down as Rooster curled up in a ball and lay down. I ran my hand down his back. "Then maybe she was lying and slipped out of the house."

"Not according to Benny and Tiffany. Benny testified that he went back to the Wallace house at exactly midnight, supposedly to have it out with James Wallace. He was positive it was midnight because the grandfather clock in the hall was chiming when he arrived. Vivian greeted him at the door and told him that her husband had just left. Now, according to the night watchmen at the country club, he noticed James Wallace's car pull up and disappear around the back of the club right when he was doing his rounds at midnight.

"Did he see anyone in the car with James?"

"No, just the car. Fifteen minutes later, he made his way around the offices and found James dead at his desk. There were two glasses in front of him, one of which had a woman's lipstick smeared on the rim. They tested the glasses and only one had strychnine in it. The other one was fine, but had Tiffany's fingerprints. In any event, even if there was someone in the car with James, it couldn't have been Vivian, because she was with Benny at the time."

"He could have been lying to cover up for her."

"And I would agree with you except that no sooner did he leave, than Tiffany showed. She arrived back at the house at the exact time the guard discovered her father's dead body. She testified that Vivian was there in her robe and nightgown, and that they talked until the police came by to inform them of James' death. So, how could Vivian poison her husband's glass at the country club if she was sitting at home the entire night?"

"Well, the same question could be asked about Tiffany? How could anyone believe she killed her father? She wouldn't have had enough time to drive with her father to the country club at midnight, poison him in his office, and then somehow get back to the house in less than fifteen minutes. The Wallace house is at least twenty minutes away from the country club. Didn't Vivian testify that she was with her?"

"She did, but she was a horrible witness. Everyone thought she was lying to protect Tiffany. She wasn't credible at all."

"What was James Wallace doing there so late at night?"

"According to Vivian and the night watchman, it wasn't unusual to find Mr. Wallace there at all sorts of hours. He was a workaholic, who practically lived in his office. If he wasn't at the country club, he was usually at the bank." Hayden leaned his hip against my desk and crossed his arms as he gazed at the board. He rubbed a hand across his eyes a few seconds later. "So, if Benny, Tiffany, and Vivian, all have alibis, where does that leave us? They were the ones that had the most to gain or lose by James' death."

I ran my hand down Rooster's back as I stared up at the ceiling. *There had to be an explanation. Something that would explain what happened to James Wallace.* I was confident that if I could just figure out who killed him, then I would know who killed Benny, despite what Vivian Wallace thought. "Let's think about this for a second. Let's suppose Rich is telling the truth and the note did point to Vivian as being James' murderer. She could have killed him any time before Benny or Tiffany arrived at midnight."

"But then how did his body get to the country club. She couldn't have driven him there, not if she was with Tiffany at the time."

"What if she had help? Someone who would clean up her mess. Someone who loved her."

"Rich?"

"It's possible. We only have his word that the note implicated Vivian. For all we know, it implicated both of them. Perhaps they were working together."

"Perhaps, they still are."

"She seemed so frightened at the hospital. I don't think she was faking it." I dropped my feet to the floor, gently set Rooster down on the ground, and then picked up my phone.

"Who are you calling?"

"Vivian. I want to know if she got her blood test back yet." I tapped my fingers against the desk impatiently as her phone rang. I was just about to hang up when Vivian finally answered.

"Wh-who is it?" asked the frightened voice on the other end of the line.

I raised my eyebrows. "Vivian? This is Kat Archer. Did you get the results of your blood test yet?"

"Yes. It came back, positive."

"Strychnine?"

I could hear the woman take a deep breath. "Yes. I showed the cops the results, but they won't listen. They won't even provide a guard."

"What did they say?"

"That they're still investigating, but . . . Rich and Dolly are still walking around. They're free and I'm a prisoner."

"Where are you?"

"At my yacht."

"You're out on the ocean?" I asked in surprise.

"No, I'm at McKinney Marina. I don't know how to operate this thing, but it's all right. I think I'm pretty safe here. As soon as I was released from the hospital, I went to the store, bought everything in sight and barricaded myself on the yacht, but . . . I didn't get enough. I'm running out of food. I just have a bottle of wine and a couple of pieces of fruit left. I'm scared. I just can't take it any more. Can you come over? I . . . I have something to say."

* * *

I pushed my hair out of my eyes as I walked toward Vivian's yacht. The wind blew my hair back across my face, and I roughly shoved it back into place. The sun had gone down and the clouds had rolled in, cutting off all moonlight. I glanced up at the small light at the end of the pier.

"What berth is she in?" Hayden asked from somewhere behind me.

"Twenty-three," I answered.

I peered up at the nearest post. "We're almost there." We walked in silence till we came to berth twenty-three and the giant yacht that Vivian was currently making her home.

"This is bigger than my apartment," I said staring up at the big ship.

"It's bigger than my house." Hayden walked to the side and called Vivian's name.

When she didn't answer, we walked to the other side, looking for a way on board. A gangplank was propped up against the yacht.

"What do you think?" I asked.

"Maybe she's in the bathroom." He stepped up on the gangplank and started to walk up. When he was finally aboard, I slowly climbed up after him, my heart lurching as the plank wobbled beneath my feet. I glanced about when my head reached the top of the railing. The yacht appeared to be deserted. A chill went down my spine. The sound of the ocean lapping against the yacht on one side, coupled with the rhythmic rocking the yacht made as it rubbed up against something on its other side, gave me a rather queasy feeling.

Hayden took my hand and dragged me the rest of the way on board. We both called out Vivian's name simultaneously, but still she didn't answer. It wasn't until we walked into the galley that we discovered why. Vivian lay on the floor clutching an empty glass. Rich Fairchild stood over her. He seemed surprised to see us. "I didn't do this. You don't understand. She called me. She said she was going to confess to killing James, and wanted me to be with her when she did. I found her like this. You have to believe me."

CHAPTER FOURTEEN

"SHE WAS LIKE a mother to me," Tiffany said as she wiped away her tears. She winced as her fingers brushed across the fading bruises around her eyes.

"Again, I'm really sorry about hitting you at the old pier," I said indicating her eyes.

"It's not your fault. It's Vivian's fault, she's the one who pushed you over the side," Tiffany said as she tipped her head back and waved her hand in front of her eyes.

I reached over to the tissue box lying on the end table and handed it to the distraught woman. Interviewing grieving family members was the part of the job I disliked most. I glanced at Tiffany in sympathy, as she noisily blew her nose. Despite everything she had learned about her stepmother, it still must hurt knowing someone you loved was dead and had tried their best to destroy your life.

"I just can't believe she killed my dad. Why would she and Rich frame me?"

"I don't know."

"At least, I know now that Benny really loved me. He was really trying to prove my innocence."

I cleared my throat. I hadn't the heart to tell her the truth. Benny Yates only cared about himself. If Vivian had accepted his marriage proposal, I'm sure he would have happily covered up her crime. It was only when she refused him yet again that he decided to call Evan and me in an attempt to expose her. Tiffany would find out soon enough, but there was no reason for me to add to her burden at this moment. I looked around at the expensive furnishings, and the giant floor to ceiling windows that provided a breathtaking view of the ocean just beyond the window. "At least this is all yours now."

Tiffany shook her head. "Vivian told me at the hospital that she was going to include me in her will, but she never did." Her lips pursed together. "It was just another lie. Her family will get everything now."

I shook my head. "The only reason you didn't inherit from your father was because you were accused and pled guilty for his murder, now that everyone knows the truth, the money should transfer back to you. You'll have to hire a lawyer, of course, but I can't see anyone denying you your rightful inheritance."

Tiffany dried her eyes with her tissue and sniffled. "I know you won't believe this, but I don't care about the money. All I wanted was justice and now I have it."

"Hmm. Yes, the woman who killed your father and framed you is now dead. As well as her accomplice," I said offhandedly.

We fell silent as I brought out my notebook and laid it on my lap. "Could I get—" I paused and shook my head as I suddenly lost track of what I was going to say. The word accomplice kept coming back to me. *Why did I say Vivian's accomplice was dead? Rich isn't dead.* "I mean now that Vivian's dead and her accomplice is in jail."

I flipped through my note pad as I thought through the facts surrounding James Wallace's death. "Did you happen to see Rich on the night your father died?"

"No, of course not. I guess he was dropping off my father's body at the country club while I was here talking to Vivian." She brought the tissue up to her face. Her body began to shake as she sobbed into her hand.

I looked down at Rich's statement. According to him, Vivian had called it off the day before James died. He had told me that he had left for Vegas later that night, and was on his way to Europe with Dolly when James died. *All easily verifiable facts. Of course, he could have been lying to me. Murderers weren't known for their honesty.* I made a note to call Luke as soon as I left Tiffany. *Surely, he can verify Rich's whereabouts the night of James' death.* I tapped my pen against my notebook.

Tiffany stopped sobbing long enough to ask me what was wrong.

"I was just thinking . . . What if Rich wasn't her accomplice?"

"Well, then, who else could have helped her kill my father?" she asked as she dropped her hand from her face.

I froze as everything suddenly became crystal clear. One name came back to me. *Benny. It had to be. Benny, Vivian's go-to boy. Benny, the one who was in love with Vivian. The one who adored her. The one who would do anything for her. The one who threatened she'd be sorry after she refused him once again. The one with $50,000 dollars in his savings account. Vivian was paying him off every month.* "Do you remember what time Benny left you at his apartment and came back over here to confront you father?" I asked, flipping back the print out of my notes.

"Yes, it was at eleven-forty. I remember hearing the door slam and checking the clock. I got worried he was going to do something stupid, so I threw on my clothes and rushed over."

I shook my head. "No, you said you woke up and found the apartment empty, and that he had left a note for you. You didn't say anything about hearing the door slam. He could have left anytime after you went to bed at ten o'clock."

"I must have forgotten. It doesn't matter. The nightmare is finally over."

"I think I know what happened now," I said slowly as I started to piece everything together. "I don't think Rich was involved."

"You don't?"

I turned to her eagerly. "This is what happened. The night of your birthday party, Benny left the apartment to go have it out with your father. But when he got there, James was already dead. Being an enterprising young man and an immoral jerk, I think he chose to help Vivian cover up the crime, instead of reporting it. More than likely, for a price, which would explain why he was always so flush with cash, to use Evan's statement. He packed up James' body, a bottle of scotch, and two glasses—making sure that one of the glasses was yours—and drove to the club. He may have hidden there until the police left a few hours later. Then shortly after the body was discovered, he went to Evan and filled his head with a bunch of lies about you."

"But . . . Benny was helping me prove my innocence. Wasn't he?" she asked.

"Only because Vivian refused him. When he realized that she was never going to marry him, and he wasn't going to get his hands on her money, he decided to punish her. That's when he called me and Evan. He was going to expose her."

"But he would have gotten in trouble. They would have charged him as a co-conspirator."

I shook my head. "It would have been his word against Vivian's. The only way she could implicate him was if she admitted to the murder. He probably figured she'd plead not guilty and keep her mouth shut. She had more to lose than he did. He just covered up the crime, but she's the one that committed it." Proud of myself, I sat back. "He knew that once you were cleared and Vivian was convicted, Wallace's fortune would revert back to you. That's why he was suddenly so interested in getting back together with you. He gave Vivian one more chance, but when she refused, he called me."

"Then that's when Vivian decided to kill him. So, Benny was just after my money all along?" she asked, as she stood and walked over to the bookcase.

"I'm sorry."

"Well, at least it's all clear now."

I started to nod, but then something occurred to me. *Chief Waltrip and everyone had assumed that Rich had been Vivian's accomplice in James' murder and poisoned Vivian after they had a falling out. But if I was right and Rich wasn't Vivian's accomplice, then who poisoned her? It couldn't have been Benny. He was already dead.* Absentmindedly, I reached for the cookie on the coffee table in front of me and began to nibble at its edges, as Tiffany chattered on about her future. *The killer and her accomplice were dead so who had a motive to kill them?* I glanced back at Tiffany who was watching me carefully as I nibbled away. Then it hit me. *There was really only one person who had motive to kill them both. The one they framed for a murder she didn't commit. The one who had lost not only a beloved father, but her inheritance and freedom as well. The one who just wanted justice and didn't trust the police or the courts.* The cookie dropped numbly from my fingers and landed in my lap. I snapped my notebook shut, trapping the cookie between the pages. *At least the cops would have something to test while I was at the hospital. If I got to the hospital.* "You know, I think I have enough for my article." I started to stand when she reached into a drawer and pulled out a gun.

"I'm so very sorry about this. I'm not a murderer. Really, I'm not."

I blew out my breath, trying to remain calm. "I believe you."

"All I wanted was justice. That's all."

"And you got it. Both of them are dead just like you wanted."

She shook her head. "No, it wasn't exactly like I wanted. I just wanted Vivian dead. I wanted her to suffer the same way she made my dad suffer. My plan was for her to die last week, but Benny ate the cookies I had poisoned instead of her. He wasn't supposed to die."

"I'm surprised, I would have thought—Oh, I understand. He was supposed to be convicted for her murder. That's why the cops found the syringe and the vial of strychnine in his apartment."

"That's right. I wanted to see him rot in jail for a murder he didn't commit. Then after he was firmly behind bars, I was going to go after Evan Quincy next. As soon as I have my inheritance, I'm going to buy that paper he works for and then I'm going to crush him. With the Herald, I can destroy anyone that helped to destroy my life." She chuckled. "Why, maybe I'll buy the Gazette, too."

"If you hate Evan so much, why did you go to the trouble of saving him?"

"Two reasons. One, I didn't even know it was Evan, and I figured that acting like a hero in front of a couple of reporters could help restore my tarnished reputation in town. And two, I want everyone to suffer in proportion to their crime. I don't actually want Evan dead. I just want to humiliate him like he humiliated me."

"How very Old Testament of you. An eye for an eye. Who else is on your hit list?"

"My lawyer, the judge, and the prosecutor, of course, but that's it. I'm not crazy, you know. I've only gone after people that have harmed me."

"But you sent a box of poisoned cookies to me. What did I do to deserve that?"

"Oh that," she said waving her hand as though it wasn't any big deal. "I didn't want Dolly to go to jail for something she didn't do like I did. She was always nice to me and had done nothing to deserve that. I thought if I sent the cookies to you with Benny's license while she was still in jail, then they would have to know she was innocent and release her. I was right, too."

"Well how nice of you. And if I died?"

Tiffany snorted. "I figured you were smart enough not to eat the cookies. Besides, I put only enough strychnine in the cookies so the cops would have something to test, but not enough to kill you just in the off chance you were an idiot."

"Thank you. What about Rich? Are you going to try to get him out of jail, too?"

Tiffany screwed up her face. "No, I don't think so. He was sleeping with my daddy's wife, you know. Maybe if he sits in jail a few years, he'll think about becoming a better person." She shook her head. "I'm sorry, Kat, killing you wasn't part of my plan, but we're just stuck with it now."

"But why? You had been doing such a good job only going after the people who hurt you, so why ruin that?"

"I'm not going to prison. No way. And frankly, you're just like Evan."

"I beg your pardon?"

"You're nosy, and you are always asking questions that are really none of your business." She looked up. "Maybe I will kill Evan too. I don't really like him." She motioned for me to stand up. When I didn't move, she shouted, "Up. Now, I can't kill you here. I don't want to ruin the carpet." She scowled as she looked around the room.

I glanced at the cookies. "You mean, they're not . . ."

"Poisoned?" She chuckled. "No, of course not. I only used strychnine because that's what Vivian had used on my dad. I got rid of it all after she died." She glanced toward the ocean. "Can you swim?"

"Yes," I said quickly. "Remember the pier?"

Tiffany made a face. "Oh, that's right."

"You're going to make a mistake. You've killed two people already. Granted, they were two horrible people, but still, you never know, the jury might be sympathetic. You'll lose whatever sympathy they may have for you if you go on a killing spree."

"I'm not going on a spree," Tiffany said scornfully. "One more person does not make it a spree."

I felt the need to object and while I was making my case, I noticed her eyes lose focus and shift toward the front door. She took a few steps away from me, giving me just enough time to grab a round decorative ball Vivian kept in a basket on the coffee table, and hide it behind my back.

Tiffany whirled around in a panic. For a second, I froze, worried that she had caught me. I was just about to hand the ball to her, when she grabbed my other arm and dragged me to the door. With my back against the door, she stuck the gun in my side and whispered a warning not to say anything, just as the doorbell rang.

I watched as Tiffany straightened her back and opened the door a few inches. "Hi, Simon."

I sighed in relief. Help had come. I didn't know how or why, but someone I knew was on the other side of the door.

"Hey, Tiffany," Simon said. "I just came by to see how you were doing. Here, I brought this for you."

Tiffany leaned back suddenly as a potted lily was thrust into her face. She spared a second to glance at me before forcefully pushing the pot back out of my view.

"That's so sweet, Simon," Tiffany said with a smile. "How very thoughtful."

"Yeah, I thought I should get you something," Simon said. "I also have a platter of food in my car for you, too. I got it from the Sea Side Shanty Inn. You know they have a great buffet. Really reasonable."

Tiffany's smile grew strained. "Wonderful, but you know I think I'm okay right now. Bye."

Simon thrust the lily forward again, preventing her from shutting the door. "I think you need to water this. It's pretty heavy. Just tell me where you want it."

Tiffany nodded. "You know, it would look great on the door step."

"Really?"

"Absolutely. That's the perfect place," she said, pointing to some place beyond my view.

"I'm really sorry about your step-mom," he said. "I can't believe she did that to you."

"Yeah, me too," Tiffany said. "Well, I really—"

"You know, I'm available if you would just like to talk."

"That's so sweet, but I just want to be alone right now."

"Yeah, I totally understand, but sometimes, it's really good to have a friend to talk to."

"I'm sorry, Simon. I'm just really tired," she said, punctuating her statement with a wide mouth yawn.

I glanced at the clock. Eleven-thirty a.m. Surely, Simon would realize something was wrong. He had to. Tiffany wasn't exactly acting normal.

"No, I completely understand," Simon said as I smothered a groan. "I would do the same thing if I was you. Just stay in and try to relax. You've been through a lot."

"I will. Bye, Simon," she said as she started to close the door.

I slumped against the door, as Tiffany slammed it shut on my hopes for a rescue. My fingers flexed around the little ceramic ball as I weighed my options. I was about to throw it in her face, when I suddenly remembered that my car was parked in front of the house. Simon had to have seen it. Surely, he'd recognize it, put two and two together and go to Hayden or Luke. Buoyed by my sudden optimistic belief that I was going to get out of this mess with my life, and a hell of a story, I allowed myself a small little smile, which fell as soon as the doorbell rang once again and I heard Simon call out, "Hey, Tiffany, it's me again. Is Kat here? Her car is out front."

In quick series of motions, Tiffany pushed me away, opened the door, and dragged Simon through the threshold.

"Oh hey, Kat," Simon said. "I thought that was your car out there." He froze when he noticed the gun in Tiffany's hand.

She glanced over at me with a shrug. "Okay, I guess now it's a spree," she shouted over Simon's wheezing. She turned to Simon who had suddenly doubled over, and circled him warily. I took her momentary lapse of concentration to throw the ball at her head. It landed against the side of her head with a dull thud, before falling to the floor, rolling over the ceramic tiles and disappearing under the couch.

She turned to look at me. "Ow," she said as she gently touched her temple. She brought her hand down and glanced at the small drop of blood on her fingers. Just then, to Tiffany's, and my surprise, Simon tackled her to the ground. The gun flew out of her hands and landed at my feet. I bent over, my fingers grazing the hilt just as Simon knocked into me, as he backed away from Tiffany. His foot collided with the gun, sliding it back to Tiffany, who was just rising to her knees.

Realizing that I was not going to be able to overcome the young woman, at least not with Simon trying to help me, I shouted, "Run," and ran to the front door.

I ran out the door as quickly as I could, surprising myself with how agile and fast I had become in such a short amount of time, as the brick driveway with its line of palm trees on either side became a blur in my peripheral vision. All I saw was the street just beyond the gate, which luckily was still open. *No one could catch me now*, I thought as I raced ahead.

A motion to my right caught my eye. Simon had overtaken me and was quickly outdistancing me. I had to admit it knocked my confidence a bit, but I pushed that aside as I passed the gate, turned the corner, and ran into an immovable force.

I spit a clump of dirt out of my mouth. Somehow, I had landed face down in a flowerbed. Strong hands lifted me up.

"Taking up track, Kat?" Luke asked in amusement.

I didn't bother to respond. I didn't know if I could. My thoughts had become nothing more than separate monosyllabic thoughts at that point. I pointed my finger toward the house. "Gun. Tiff. Go," I ordered before rising unsteadily to my feet. I was happy to note, Luke had already unholstered his weapon, and was making his way to the house by the time I was in a standing position.

EPILOGUE

THE PLANT STAND came down with a crash, sending the potted fern rolling toward the door. Rooster paused in his hunt, torn before attacking the fern, or continuing to chase whatever he had spotted hiding behind the filing cabinet. He watched the fern for a few seconds before dashing under the desk.

I picked my feet up. A few seconds later, Rooster jumped up onto the desk, sending papers and the phone flying to the floor. I lifted my hands off the keyboard as he raced across the desk and flew off the side. He continued across the office, his paws barely touching the floor before I lost sight of him. A few seconds later, I heard the sound of a thump, followed by the shaking of a filing cabinet.

Hayden shook his head. "That's my little hunter."

"Don't worry. Rooster Cogburn always gets his mouse."

Hayden groaned. "That's real clever, Kat. About as clever as your headline." He walked over to Rooster and picked him up. Lifting him up to eye level, he checked him over for any injuries. Finding none, he set the cat down on the cat bed we kept in the corner of the office.

"What's wrong with my headline?"

He raised an eyebrow. "A Murder Spree Prevented. A bit sensationalist, don't you think?"

"A spree perfectly describes what was about to happen. Thank God, Luke showed up when he did. You should have seen it. Tiffany came running out of her house pointing her gun. They actually had a standoff for a few minutes. I was sure she was going to start shooting at any moment."

"What were you doing while this was happening?"

"Wishing I had my camera."

Hayden grinned. "And that's why you're my best reporter."

Taken aback, my mouth fell open. "Really?"

"You may be a horrible food critic—absolutely awful—"

I snapped my mouth shut and crossed my arms. "Do I hear a but . . . ?"

"But you're an excellent investigative reporter."

"Thank you. So, about my food column—"

Hayden smiled. "It's still yours until we get someone new."

Hayden was nothing, if not stubborn.

"Yippee." Luckily, I was just as stubborn. I opened my mouth to complain when he nodded enthusiastically.

"I figured you would be happy about that. Now, keep going. What happened at the standoff? How did it end?"

"With good ole southern charm. Luke poured it on thick. Of course, it helped that he had a gun pointed at her head, but I still think it was just an overload of charm that finally convinced her to lower her gun and give up."

"Charm?" he asked in disappointment.

"Yep. He can be very charismatic when he wants to be."

I watched curious as his smile slowly fell from his face. He ran a hand across his jaw. "How well do you know Detective Casey?"

Surprised by the sudden change of subject, I said, "A few years."

"Were you two—?"

Whatever he was about to ask, was lost as the door opened and the aforementioned Detective Casey walked in. Swaggered probably more accurately reflected the motion, but at any rate, he came in, and walked up to my desk. "Well, speak of the devil, if it isn't Detective Casey. Is this a social call, Detective?"

Luke pulled up a chair next to my desk. "Business, actually. I thought you would want to know that Tiffany confessed to everything. She was very forthcoming."

"Good," I said, reaching for my pen and notepad. "When will she be arraigned?"

"Tomorrow morning."

"I have some questions," I said balancing my notepad on my crossed legs.

Luke groaned. "I figured you would."

"First of all, how in the world did you know that I was at Tiffany's?"

"I didn't. I went to Tiffany's because I wanted to talk to her again. I just had a gut feeling that Rich wasn't the one that had killed Vivian and since Tiffany seemed to be at the center of everything that had happened in the last couple of weeks, I decided to pay her a visit."

"No kidding." I glanced over Luke's head as Hayden hovered nearby. "When I spoke to Vivian, she said she had barricaded herself on the yacht. Did Tiffany say how she was able to kill her?"

"She followed Vivian after she left the hospital the other day," Luke said. "When she realized that Vivian was going to hide out on the yacht, she decided to beat her to it. She hid on the yacht and waited for Vivian to board. Once Vivian was settled in for the night, she snuck into the galley and poisoned the bottle of wine. Then it was just a matter of waiting for her to take a drink."

Hayden sat down at Simon's desk. "How did Tiffany figure out that Vivian had killed her father, and that Benny had helped her?"

"Tiffany said that she began to suspect Vivian at her trial. She felt that Vivian helped the prosecution more than the defense with her testimony, but it wasn't until the day before Valentine's Day that she knew for sure. Vivian was apparently concerned that Benny was about to betray her, and was trying to get confirmation that her secret was still safe. Tiffany overheard them talking. She said she didn't even think twice. She immediately set her plan in motion."

"Why did she put the poison in Dolly's cookies?" I asked.

"They were handy. Simon left them on the table at the Cookie Jar while they were talking. When he turned away for a few seconds, she dropped the bag on the ground behind a plant. Then once they were walking back to his apartment, she made an excuse, dashed back to the store and picked them up. She knew Vivian had been trying to get her hands on them, and figured it would be easy to put the poison into the gooey center."

"Poor Dolly," I said. "She's still upset about the whole thing and is considering scrapping the entire recipe. I think she was living in denial until they found Vivian's body. She says they leave a bad taste in her mouth now."

Luke glanced at his watch. "Well, I've got to go."

"Hey, I have more questions."

"Save them," he said rising to his feet, "I have places I have to be."

"Really?" I asked. "Do you have anything you want to share with the fourth estate?"

He paused at the doorway and grinned. "Have I ever?" he asked before closing the door behind him.

"See," I said pointing to the door in irritation. "Charming. Like a snake."

"Hmm, well," Hayden said, leaning forward and balancing his elbows on his knees. He clasped his hands between his legs and smiled. "I'm just glad you are okay." He paused and cleared his throat. "And Simon. I'm glad you and Simon made it out okay." He waved his hand toward my computer, his handsome face twisting into a grimace. "But re-write your headline. This is a reputable paper you know." He stood up and started toward his office before turning around suddenly at his doorway. "Oh, by the way, the community center is having a bake off tonight. Fried frog legs. Have fun," he said, shutting the door quickly behind him.

I turned back to my computer and deleted my headline. Propping my head on hand, I tapped my fingers on my desk until inspiration struck. "Showdown at the Wallace House of Horrors," I wrote with a smile. I hit send and leaned back as Rooster jumped on my desk and lay down on my keyboard. "Much less sensational, don't you think?"

The End

Made in the USA
Lexington, KY
26 June 2014